FINN
AND THE
INTERGALACTIC LUNCHBOX

ALSO BY MICHAEL BUCKLEY

The Sisters Grimm series

The NERDS series

FINN
AND THE
INTERGALACTIC
LUNCHBOX

MICHAEL BUCKLEY

DELACORTE PRESS

Text copyright © 2020 by Michael Buckley
Jacket art copyright © 2020 by Petur Antonsson

All rights reserved. Published in the United States by Delacorte Press, an imprint of Random House Children's Books, a division of Penguin Random House LLC, New York.

Delacorte Press is a registered trademark and the colophon is a trademark of Penguin Random House LLC.

Visit us on the Web! rhcbooks.com

Educators and librarians, for a variety of teaching tools, visit us at RHTeachersLibrarians.com

Library of Congress Cataloging-in-Publication Data
Names: Buckley, Michael, author.
Title: Finn and the intergalactic lunchbox / Michael Buckley.
Description: First edition. | New York : Delacorte Press, [2020] | Summary:
"When Earth is threatened by an invading race of bugs called the Plague,
11-year-old Finn, his arch-nemesis, Lincoln, his crush, Julep, and one pink
unicorn lunchbox become Earth's last best hope against destruction"
— Provided by publisher.
Identifiers: LCCN 2019007842 | ISBN 978-0-525-64687-7 (hc) |
ISBN 978-0-525-64688-4 (lib. bdg.) | ISBN 978-0-525-64689-1 (ebook)
Subjects: | CYAC: Extraterrestrial beings—Fiction. | Insects—Fiction. |
Lunchboxes—Fiction. | Science fiction.
Classification: LCC PZ7.B882323 Fin 2020 | DDC [Fic]—dc23

The text of this book is set in 11.25-point New Century Schoolbook LT Pro.
Interior design by Vikki Sheatsley

Printed in the United States of America
10 9 8 7 6 5 4 3 2 1
First Edition

For Finn,
the hero of
all my stories

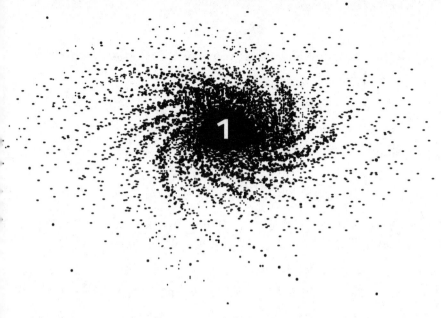

1

"**W**ell, this got exciting pretty quick," Dax Dargon said to her robot partner, Highbeam. They were crouched behind a dumpster with shock blasts and sonic grenades exploding in the dead end alley around them. Every *Ka-pow!* scrambled Highbeam's digital face. Each time it returned to normal, his frown was bigger.

"Never a dull moment with you, Dax," the robot grumbled as a sonic grenade sailed overhead and crashed into the building behind them. Concrete sprayed into the air.

Dax pulled her bandanna over her mouth and nose and waited for the dust to settle. It was tragic what the Plague was doing to her city. Her dad used to bring her here to shop in the street markets when she was little. Now it was a war zone.

"You don't blame me for this mess, do you?"

"Let me see. You stole a top-secret weapon from the Plague mothership in broad daylight. Yes, I think this is your fault."

"I didn't have a choice, big guy. You heard what those guards were saying about this thing." Dax wriggled out of her pack and dug around inside it until she found the object at the center of all the excitement. It was no bigger than a sheet of paper, thick and made from a hard transparent substance. Inside it, circuitry and lights blinked and zipped around like snow bees. Dax had seen a lot of odd things since joining the Resistance, but nothing like this.

"They called it a wormhole generator," Highbeam grumbled. "And it sounds like trouble."

"They also said it could break the back of the Resistance. The Plague could send troops anywhere in a flash without warning. We couldn't defend ourselves," Dax said.

"Well, a heads-up would have been nice," Highbeam said. "Or maybe a discussion about a plan and an escape route. They've got us pinned down in this alley."

"Aww, buddy. You sound like one of those boring old robots that putter around the park," Dax said. "We're spies. This is part of the job description. What happened to the Highbeam Silverman, who was always ready for adventure?"

"I'm *not* old—but I'd like to be someday! Unfortunately, my kid partner keeps getting us into trouble." He fired a couple of shots from his hand cannon before ducking back down.

"Don't call me a kid," Dax hissed, rising to spray the alley with her shocker. "I'm going to be thirteen soon!"

"In a year and two months, and that's looking less and less likely. You noticed the bright yellow warnings painted on the side of this dumpster we're using as a shield, right?"

Dax focused on the words and gasped.

"This thing is full of fusion waste! Who would leave this in the street?"

"Probably some scavenger trying to sell it. One lucky shot from those soldiers and we're all going sky high!"

"Attention, blue-skinned criminal and robot sidekick!" A commanding voice at the other end of the alley silenced the shooting.

"Sidekick?" Highbeam cried. "I'm not a sidekick!"

"My name is Major Sin Kraven of the Plague High Guard. You have stolen property that belongs to the armada. We have you surrounded. You cannot escape. I urge you to use your tiny, primitive brains and surrender. If you cooperate, I offer a rare act of mercy."

"This ought to be good," Dax whispered to Highbeam. She cupped her hand and shouted, "We're listening!"

"Your deaths will be quick. When my people lay their eggs inside your body, you will not suffer. Our offspring will grow inside you, feasting on your internal meats. Once they are strong enough, they will claw their way out of your corpse and join our ranks."

"How is that merciful?" Dax shouted.

"We prefer to lay our eggs inside a living person and keep them that way until our hoppers hatch," Kraven explained.

Highbeam cringed.

"I'm going to need some time to think about it!" Dax yelled.

"You have three minutes!" Kraven said.

Highbeam poked his head over the top of the dumpster. "I assume we're passing on his offer. I count ten soldiers, but I'm sure there are more on the way," he reported. "Here's the plan: I'm going to go out there and break some heads. While they're bleeding all over the street, you take the gizmo and make a run for it. Got it? Good. *Demolition mode.*"

A yellow warning light on the robot's chest flashed and Highbeam's head sank between his shoulders like he was an enormous steel turtle. He cracked his robot knuckles and moved to stand, but Dax held his arm.

"They'll blow you apart. We're going to have to try something else."

"What else can we do? Oh, no! You've got that look in your eye."

"What look?" she asked.

"The look you give me when we're about to do something dumb!"

Dax dismissed him with a wave of her hand. Her attention was already on the stolen weapon.

"Can you link to this thing? Maybe there are some instructions buried inside it."

Highbeam's head returned to normal. His frown was even bigger, but he didn't argue. A low humming sound came out of his chest, and a moment later a bell chime told them he had succeeded.

"Uh-oh! Dax, this is Alcherian, which means it's complicated and dangerous. We shouldn't mess with it."

"Alcherian? Then what the guards said was true," she said. "When the Plague destroyed Alcheria, they captured scientists, and now they are forcing them to build weapons. This thing must be the real deal. How do I turn it on?"

"Dax, you're not thinking what I think you're thinking, are you?"

"I probably am," she admitted.

"Forget it!"

"Two minutes!" Kraven shouted.

"Highbeam! We're running out of time," Dax cried. "Where's the on button?"

"Fine! You have to shake it," he grumbled.

It sounded silly, but Dax did as she was told and watched the sheet unfold in her hands like an intricate origami. It formed a cube, complete with a control panel and a view-screen on one side. A murky red planet floated there, as well as a cascade of information about its atmosphere, population, and vegetation.

"What's this?" Dax said, eyeing it closely.

"This thing has info on every known planet in the universe," Highbeam explained.

Dax studied the red planet. It was practically one giant volcano. It wouldn't work for her plan, but if Highbeam was right, she guessed the arrow buttons under the screen would give her another option. The red planet vanished, and a yellow world covered in endless deserts took its place. It was too close to its sun. The next planet was far too close to the Plague home world. The next was littered with craters and barely had an atmosphere. The next was being dragged into a black hole.

"One minute!" Kraven shouted.

Suddenly, a tiny blue globe appeared in the screen. It had green continents and wide oceans. There wasn't much information about it, only that its population was primitive compared to her world. They hadn't even achieved interstellar travel, but it was on the far side of the universe, in a galaxy called the Milky Way about as far as you could get from the Plague. It was perfect.

"How do I log in coordinates?"

"Type in the location number on the keypad, but really, Dax! We should not test-drive a technology this complicated. We could end up inside a sun, or freezing to death on an ice planet. Dax? Are you listening to me? No, of course you're not listening to me."

Her fingers typed in the coordinates. "Target Lock: Earth" appeared on the screen, and a blue button flashed the words "Open Tunnel." She was about to push it, when Highbeam stopped her.

"Whoa! Slow down! You have to log in a specific location," Highbeam said. "If you don't, there's no way of knowing where the wormhole will open."

"Your time is up, blue skin!" Kraven shouted. "What is your answer?"

"Sorry, partner. Looks like we are out of time." Dax pushed the blue button. Her ears were pounded by a strange booming sound, like water rushing through a tube, only louder than anything she had ever heard. A blinding light followed from the top of the box, and for a moment neither Dax nor Highbeam could see or hear anything. When their eyes and ears finally adjusted, they found something strange materializing in front of them. A hole in space hovered above the cube, as if someone had taken a knife and sliced open reality. Inside it was a swirling whirlpool. Stars, planets, asteroids, and comets spun around in it like ingredients in a blender. It was the most beautiful and bewildering thing either of them had ever seen.

Unfortunately, the lights and noise alerted Kraven and his soldiers and their attack resumed, only this time with twice the savagery. Debris from explosions rained down, some of it landing dangerously close to the two spies. *Whoosh!* A grenade hit the ground so close to the dumpster it nearly toppled over onto Dax and Highbeam.

"You've gone and made them mad, Dax!" Highbeam said, returning fire. "Hop into the hole. I'll fight them off as long as I can."

"Not me, big guy. You." Dax reached up to the base of the robot's spine. There her fingers found a lever that released Highbeam's limbs. His body collapsed into a pile of parts.

"I shouldn't have told you about the lever," he moaned.

"You're going on a very important mission," she said as she hefted one of his legs into the whirlpool. It vanished in an instant.

"Dax, wait! The instructions say sending technology into a wormhole is a big no-no. The radiation can damage it. In case you forgot: *I'm technology!* My circuit board could get barbecued. I could come out missing a leg or even my head! I need my head, Dax!"

"You'll be fine," she said, shoving his arms into the tunnel. "You're the toughest robot in the Resistance and the only one I trust to keep this weapon safe. When you get to Earth, take the machine and lie low. I'll send someone to pick you up as soon as I can."

"Wait! You're not coming with me?"

"I've got to stay behind to throw the generator in," she said as a grenade vaporized a parked transport pod.

"Dax, that's an even bigger no-no! The instructions say so in all caps! DO NOT SEND THE GENERATOR INTO ITS OWN WORMHOLE. It's serious when it's in all caps."

Dax picked up Highbeam's head. She gave his shiny digital face a kiss.

"Be safe and with any luck I'll see you soon. Long live the fight. Long live the Resistance!"

"Dax! No!"

She hurled his head into the tunnel and watched it sink into the cosmic soup. With explosions growing closer, she scooped up the generator and prepared to throw it in as well, but a shock blast landed mere inches from her and sent her flailing. She crashed hard on the ground, dazed and in searing pain. She staggered to her feet, and *BOOM!* She was rocked by another explosion. Her brain bounced around her skull. She couldn't tell up from down, but what she had to do was still clear as daylight. The Plague could not have this weapon. So with all the strength she had left, she threw it. *FLASH!* Electricity shot out of the wormhole and sent her tumbling. Her back slammed against the fusion dumpster. Agony swam up her spine and into her head. She struggled to stay conscious, and as black spots danced in her eyes, Dax saw the whirlpool shrink, smaller and smaller, until there was no evidence it had ever existed.

Enraged soldiers surrounded her. They shoved their weapons into her chest and dragged her to her feet. Sin Kraven pushed to the front and stood so close his face was inches from her own. She tried not to look at him, knowing all her courage would melt away.

Dax was a spy. She and Highbeam infiltrated the Plague's ships and worked side by side with them, pretending to be traitors to their own people, but she never got used to what they looked like: the sharp, spindly limbs, the snapping mandibles, the hard yellow skin as strong as steel. Their wings were huge and agitated, and their hands were nothing more than gnarled claws. But it was their eyes that turned her blood to ice. Huge. Black. And empty. Her nightmares were always the same—falling into the eyes and discovering they had no bottom.

"You have one chance to tell me where you sent our weapon, blue skin," Kraven said as he rubbed his back legs together. It created a snapping sound that rattled her teeth. The rest of his soldiers joined him, creating a deafening orchestra. Even putting her hands over her ears could not drown it out. "Tell me . . . or we will lay our eggs in you while you are still alive."

2

"HOW MANY CHANCES HAVE I GIVEN YOU?" Principal Doogan's meaty fist came down hard on his desk. It sent his World's Greatest Principal coffee mug skittering across his desk and toward the floor. Finn caught it before it shattered. He offered it back, hoping it might win him some mercy, but no. Mr. Doogan snatched the mug without a thank-you, then cradled it in his hands like it was a precious treasure.

"Too many, if you ask me," Lincoln said. The shaggy-haired boy was slumped in his chair, staring at the dusty ceiling fan above. Finn was stunned. Who would be disrespectful at a time like this? Couldn't Lincoln see the throbbing red veins on Mr. Doogan's forehead? The man was about to explode.

"Too many is right!" Doogan roared. "You two have

been in my office almost every day since you showed up at this school, and to be honest, I'm tired of looking at you. Why can't you get along?"

Finn quietly raged. This wasn't his fault. He went to class. He did his homework. He kept his head down and he stayed out of trouble, just like he promised. Was it his fault that a psychopath waited for him before and after school to beat him up? The fact that Finn didn't fight back should have told the principal he was trying to be a good kid, but it seemed no matter what he did, trouble found him. It wasn't fair.

"I think there's been a misunderstanding, Mr. Doogan," Finn said. He swallowed his pride and did his best to sound sincere. "Lincoln and I get along great! We're practically best friends."

"When I found you outside, Mr. Sidana had you in a headlock. He was making you punch your face with your own fist."

"Boys being boys," Finn said, throwing in a chuckle.

"Mr. Sidana, how much of this story is true?" the principal asked.

"Zero percent."

"I'll say one thing for you, Lincoln, I always get the truth out of you," Mr. Doogan said, then cast his steely eyes on Finn. "Unlike Mr. Foley, who will say whatever he thinks I want to hear."

"Maybe that's why I keep wanting to punch him,

Mr. Doogan. I always thought it was his face," Lincoln said.

The principal pushed back from his desk and crossed the room to a coffee maker resting on a little table. He took a deep snort from the pot, grimaced, then poured himself a cup anyway.

"What am I going to do with you two?"

"Last time you said you would expel us if we got into another fight," Lincoln said. "Unless you were bluffing."

Finn palmed his face in disbelief. Something was wrong with Lincoln Sidana's brain.

"I wasn't bluffing." He riffled through a file cabinet until he found a couple of yellow forms with the words "Recommendation for Expulsion" printed at the top.

Panic swirled in Finn's belly. This was exactly what he had been trying to avoid. His mom would be crushed.

"Give us another chance," he begged.

"You have pushed me into a corner. You're in trouble almost every day. I reached out to your mother, Finn. I never heard back from her."

"She works," Finn mumbled, but the truth was he deleted Mr. Doogan's emails before she got a chance to read them. Mom didn't have a clue what was going on at school.

"That's unfortunate, Mr. Foley, because she might have been helpful," Mr. Doogan said.

"There has to be a way we can fix this!" Finn cried.

"Who is 'we'? Have you got a mouse in your pocket?" Lincoln said.

"Fine. Tell me how *I* can fix it," Finn said. "I can learn to get along with him. I could even be . . . his friend."

Doogan studied the boys as if they were a complicated math problem, then gazed into his coffee mug as if the answer might be floating there. Suddenly, he smiled.

"Okay. One last chance, but if it doesn't work I'll personally pack up your lockers."

"Thank you," Finn blurted out.

"Don't thank me yet. You're not going to like what you have to do to earn it. When I was a kid, I used to fight with my brothers twenty-four hours a day," Doogan admitted, "and when we pushed our mom too far, she made us sit in our bedroom and we weren't allowed out until we could get along."

"Not allowed out?" Finn asked.

"Not allowed out," Doogan repeated firmly. "Until you are friends."

"Friends?" Lincoln laughed.

"If you can make it happen by the end of the day, I'll tear these forms up and we'll forget this ever happened, but your friendship has to be real. No bologna, Foley! That's my offer. Take it or leave it."

"We'll take it." Finn tried to sound excited, but it came out defeated.

Doogan seemed satisfied. He drained his coffee mug and set it down. "All right, then. I've got a school to run," he said. "Good luck, gentlemen."

A moment later he was gone and Finn and Lincoln were all alone.

It was silent in Mr. Doogan's office for a very long time. It was just fine with Finn. He needed the time to wrap his head around the deal he made. He hated Lincoln and Lincoln hated him. How were they supposed to build a friendship?

After thirty minutes he still didn't have an answer, but the clock wasn't waiting around for him to figure one out. If there was any chance of saving their butts, they had to get started. He turned his chair to face Lincoln.

"Forget it," Lincoln said before Finn could utter a word.

"If we talk to each other, we'll probably find we have something in common, and—"

"Do you hear the words coming out of your mouth hole?" Lincoln said.

Finn sighed. "Then let's fake it."

"I'm not going to lie for you," Lincoln said.

"Then lie for yourself!"

Lincoln shook his head.

"You bully me every day but lying is against your moral code?" Finn cried. "He's going to kick us out of school."

"Then I guess we will have something in common."

Lincoln put his head on the desk, signaling that he was done talking. Soon the office was filled with the soft buzz of his snores. The bully was sound asleep.

Finn gawked at him in disbelief. Lincoln Sidana was going to ruin his life.

3

Anxious hours passed, and Finn spent them plotting ways out of his troubles. Meanwhile, Lincoln slept as if he didn't have a worry in the world. It was only when the bell rang for lunch that he fell to the floor, startled. Embarrassed, he kicked his chair as if it were to blame. Finn might have laughed if he hadn't been so angry.

While Lincoln fought with the furniture, Finn wandered to the window to get some fresh air. Mr. Doogan had quite a view. Outside, the town of Cold Spring stretched before him, with Bear Mountain guarding the horizon. Its hills were blanketed with firs and oaks. Not far away, the Hudson River rolled toward the Atlantic. Orange and crimson leaves fell through the neighborhoods. An ice cream truck coasted through the streets. Everything was beautiful, like something on a postcard.

Finn hated it.

He hated every street and corner, every store, every tree and slope, every ripple in the river. Cold Spring wasn't his home. You can't call a place you're stuck in *home,* and Finn was stuck. In Cold Spring he was the new kid, the weird kid, the friendless kid, not like his old hometown of Garrison. He missed his friends and his swimming pool and his old house, where everyone was happy and there was no one waiting outside the school to punch him in the ear.

Finn watched kids spill onto the lawn, where they unpacked sandwiches and fruit cups and squeezable yogurts. Their chatter and laughter drifted up to the window and made him sad. Back at his old school he had more friends than he could count, but then Dad walked out on the family and Mom moved Finn and his sister Kate to a rental that was falling down around them. They didn't know a soul in Cold Spring, and Finn intended to keep it that way. What was the point of getting to know anyone? Everyone abandoned him in the end.

Only, there was one person he couldn't ignore. She had long brown hair and glasses that magnified her eyes into moons. Every day she sat beneath one of the oak trees on the school lawn and buried her nose in a book. Her name was Julep Li. Sometimes when Finn looked at her, he felt happy and barfy at the same time. He wasn't sure why, but the queasiness happened every time she smiled. Oh, and when she spoke in her honey-soaked Southern accent. And when she pushed her glasses up. But mostly when he saw the books she read. Julep Li had the weirdest taste in books:

> *Bigfoot Encounters of the Northeastern United States*
>
> *Legends of the Black-Eyed Children*
>
> *How to Fend off Psychic and Mystic Attacks*
>
> *What's at the Bottom of a Black Hole?*

Every day there was a new book, and every day Finn was more fascinated with their reader. *Yes,* he told himself, *it had to be the books.*

"Who are you looking at, derp?" Lincoln said, suddenly appearing next to him at the window.

Finn did his best not to react. The last thing in the world he wanted was for Lincoln to find out he was interested in Julep Li. Lincoln would tease him until it didn't feel good to think about her anymore.

"Why do you call everyone a derp?" Finn said, trying to change the subject.

"I don't. Just the derps, derp!" Lincoln said. "Any more stupid questions you need answered?"

"Yeah! Why are you trying to get me kicked out of school?"

Lincoln rolled his eyes.

"Not everything is about you," he said. "And so what if you get kicked out? The world isn't going to end. I've been kicked out of a million schools. You'll just go to another one—probably a better one."

Before Finn could argue, the office door opened and Assistant Principal Applebaum entered. Her hair was fire-engine red, and she wore sweaters with cats on them all year round. She gave the boys her best disappointed look, but her face was so used to smiling she couldn't make it happen.

"How are you getting along?" she asked.

"It would be easier if he would stop being a loser, but he's stubborn," Lincoln said.

"Oh, boys. I hope you're taking this seriously. I've never seen Mr. Doogan so upset," she said. "I heard him yelling all the way down in the library."

"I'm doing my best," Finn said.

"Maybe something to eat will help. I brought your lunches from your backpacks." She handed Lincoln a brown paper sack with his name scrawled on it in marker, then turned to Finn with . . . well, it was technically a lunchbox. It had a zipper and a handle, but the rest of it was horrible. Decorated in pastel pink and covered in glitter and rainbows, it featured two happy unicorns on the front with the words *Unicorn Magic* written in cotton-candy clouds.

Finn was horrified. This wasn't his lunchbox—it was his sister Kate's! How did it end up in his backpack? His thoughts raced back to that morning. His mom forgot to set her phone alarm, and everyone woke up forty-five minutes late. They ran around like maniacs trying to get ready for school. Mom begged him to pack his and Kate's lunches as she sprinted past him toward the shower. Of course, his little sister had to insert some drama to make everything harder.

"I can't find my tights," Kate said.

"I saw a pair on your dresser," he said as he sliced an apple.

"Are you serious? Are you really saying that to me? Those are kitten tights. Kittens are for babies!" Kate said, as if it were a known fact throughout the universe. "I need my unicorn tights."

"Everything was kittens last week."

"That was *last week*!"

"They're in your top drawer," he said. "I put them away when I did *your* laundry, which is ridiculous. You're eight years old. You can help around the house."

"They're not in my drawer! I looked."

"I'll bet you a million dollars they are," Finn said.

"You don't have a million dollars," Kate said.

"I won't need it."

"You better go to the bank!" she shouted as she spun around and stomped up the stairs. "Because you're going to owe me a million dollars."

Mom darted into the kitchen wearing her robe and a towel wrapped around her head.

"Never a dull moment around here, huh?" she said as she poured herself a cup of coffee. "What's Kate yelling about?"

"Kittens and unicorns." Finn cut the crusts off his sister's sandwich. She didn't deserve a brother as great as him.

"I'm not paying you!" Kate said when she reappeared in the kitchen, wearing the tights.

That was when it must have happened. He was so distracted, he shoved the lunchboxes into the wrong backpacks. Aaarggh! Who needed Lincoln to ruin his life when he was doing a great job all on his own?

Lincoln eyed the lunchbox and bent over laughing.

"Don't tease him, Mr. Sidana. It takes a lot of bravery to be yourself. Finn doesn't care what other people think, and I'm impressed." Assistant Principal Applebaum placed the lunchbox in Finn's hands. "You be you."

Finn wanted to tell her she was wrong. He cared very much what people thought. His real lunchbox was blue, regular, plain, and free of glitter, cotton-candy clouds, and most importantly, unicorns! But Ms. Applebaum smiled, and before he knew it she was gone.

Lincoln, however, was in his face. He snatched the lunchbox away and turned it over and over, studying every side. "Well, well, well. Isn't this something?"

"It belongs to my sister. Give it back." Finn tried to yank it away, but Lincoln moved out of his reach.

"Don't get handsy. Oh, look at these unicorns. They're so happy prancing around in their rainbow meadow. Which of them do you like best? Is it the one with the ribbon in her mane, or is it the one with the star tattoo on her butt? How can you choose? They've both stolen my heart."

"Very funny. Hand it over. I'm serious."

"Calm down! How can anyone be so salty when they own this lunchbox? It's happiness with a handle and you can put a sammich in it! Do sparkles shoot out when you open the thermos?"

Frustrated, Finn snatched Lincoln's sack lunch.

"Fine! I'll eat your lunch." He thrust his hand inside the bag, reached around, and pulled out a pair of tighty-whities. "What in the world is this?"

Lincoln's mischievous grin melted like ice cream on a hot day. He lunged for the underpants, but Finn was too quick and darted behind Mr. Doogan's desk. He waved the underwear like a flag.

"Don't get handsy," he mocked. "Now, look at this. I have so. Many. Questions. First, should you be eating underwear for lunch? I'm not sure this is very nutritious. Is it in the fruit group, or is it a dairy? Wait, maybe the label will tell me. It says 'Husky Boy.' Is that what you are, Lincoln? Are you a husky boy? Well, you be you. Hey! I hope these are clean!"

Enraged, Lincoln torpedoed himself across the desk and grabbed Finn's shirt. The two tumbled to the floor and rolled around, kicking and punching one another.

"Why can't you leave me alone?" Finn cried. "I'm trying to stay out of trouble!"

"Because I can't stand your big dumb head!" Lincoln shouted.

The fight might have gone on all day if not for the sudden and surprising noise. It sounded like a flush, as if the universe had just used the toilet, and it was loud enough to shake the windows. Weirder still, it came from inside the glittery, pink, rainbow-covered unicorn lunchbox.

With a yelp, the boys threw it across the room and cowered behind the principal's desk.

"Dude," Lincoln whispered. "What did your mother pack you for lunch?"

Finn peeked over the desk and saw the lunchbox levitating off the floor, hovering as if held up by invisible hands.

"There's a ghost in your lunchbox, derp."

"There's no such thing as ghosts, stupid."

"Don't call me stupid!" Lincoln grabbed Finn by the throat and the fight resumed until the lunchbox abruptly fell to the floor. Its zipper slid aside, and when the lid popped open, untamed electric tendrils shot out and whipped around the room, scorching everything they touched.

"What do we do?" Finn shouted over the noise.

"Close the lid!" Lincoln yelled.

"Why me?"

"It's your lunchbox!"

Finn crawled toward the chaos. The sound and energy was so intense it felt like a physical force. It pushed him back two inches for every one he moved forward. Just when his fingers were within inches of the lid, something flew out. It smacked him hard in the chest. It didn't hurt but it did surprise him, because suddenly he was overwhelmed by a flood of information bombarding his brain.

Images and facts about every corner of space invaded his thoughts. Planets he had never heard of flashed in his eyes, along with endless streams of data about their civilizations, histories, environments, resources, and military might. Along with the info came portraits of alien life-forms. Most of them didn't look remotely human—creatures with no bones, bodies made of ice, beings with fire for hair. There were giants lumbering across continents and entire cities where the tallest inhabitant was no bigger than an inch in height. There was a world full of ostriches, driving around in tiny cars, and a moon where everyone lived underwater.

None of this can be real, he told himself. He must have hit his head in the fight. He was probably asleep, dreaming all this, even the strange hole he saw forming above the lunchbox. It was so bright and beautiful he could barely look at it. And what was inside the hole? Were those stars?

He reached out toward the lunchbox. The second his fingers touched the handle, there was a *flash*! Finn was jerked off his feet and sucked into the hole, and he no longer felt like he was dreaming. This was real! Mr. Doogan's office, Lincoln, the lunchbox, his school, Cold Spring, and Earth disappeared behind him as he rocketed into space. Finn found himself inside a tunnel of light, zipping past white-hot suns and glowing nebulas. He flew around the remains of a massive red planet cracked in half by an ancient collision. He dipped into the ring of a mysterious world, leaving a streak of silver dust trailing behind him.

And he screamed.

A lot.

The tunnel took him to a strange green planet, where he suddenly went into a nosedive and fell through clouds, certain he would *splat* on the ground at any second. Just before he crashed, he came to an abrupt stop in an alleyway. Abandoned vehicles were parked along the street, and there was rubble and smoke everywhere he looked.

The word "Nemeth" appeared in his mind, and somehow he understood that it was this world's name.

There was little time to try to understand what had just happened. At the end of the alley was a group of grasshoppers shuffling around in military uniforms. Each had tough yellow exoskeletons, six gangly legs, a vicious whipping tail, and a set of wings, just like the ones he saw in his backyard.

Only these were six feet tall.

Their faces were flat and featureless with twitching antennae on top, mandibles, and gaping black eyes. They noticed his arrival and aimed their weapons at him.

"Don't move!" one of them screeched. He wore a black jacket emblazoned with a silver badge. Its language was nothing more than clicks and gurgles, but Finn seemed to understand the same way he understood where he was. The bug pressed his face close to Finn's. It had red markings on it.

"What grotesque creature are you?" the bug demanded as he pressed his weapon against Finn's temple. "A spy from some other worthless world, I suppose. Your tiny Resistance is testing my patience today. Where have your partners taken our weapon? And before you speak, you should know that if you lie to me, I'm going to add another hole to your face."

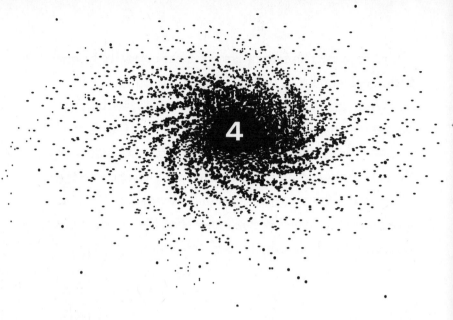

4

After watching Finn get sucked into a hole in the air, Lincoln was determined not to let it happen to him. He made his way for the door, only to be stopped in his tracks when something shot out of the tear and streaked past him. It was a silver blur, ricocheting off two walls and the ceiling, and traveling so fast he couldn't make out what it was until it landed at his feet. He realized it was a head—at least, it was shaped like a head, but it was made out of metal, with a glass screen for a face. Tiny glowing symbols marched across it until they swirled into identical circles; then they blinked.

"No! Dax!" a gruff voice shouted. "Wait! Am I here? Is this Earth? Who are *zzzack* you? Whoa! What was *zzzeeeck* that? Blast it! I'm glitching!"

Startled, Lincoln punted the head across the room.

Fwap! Into the trash can, just as more silver body parts arrived: a foot, a leg, an arm, and a hand. They smashed furniture and light fixtures and demolished Mr. Doogan's computer. An out-of-control butt smashed his coffee mug into pieces.

"Not cool, kid! *Zzzack!*" the head shouted from the trash can.

A static charge filled the air, and Lincoln felt his hair stand on end. All at once the body parts zipped toward one another and assembled into a seven-foot robot with a barrel chest, long, thick cables for arms, and a very big weapon strapped to its hip. All it was missing was its head. Lincoln watched in stunned silence as it lumbered to the trash can and retrieved it, jamming it into place between its shoulders.

"You're a robot," Lincoln whispered.

"Winner, winner, chicken dinner," the robot said with a snarl. It gave itself a shake like a wet dog and then turned back to the boy. "All right, kid. I ought to ring your bell for booting my noggin across the room, but I'm on an important mission. Tell me where the gizmo is and I'll let you go without a scratch."

"Gizmo?" Lincoln repeated.

"Yeah, it looks like a glowing box. It should have come through the wormhole before me," the robot said.

"Haven't seen it," Lincoln said. "But I did see a hole swallow a kid."

"It did what?" the robot said as it stomped toward Lincoln, but before he could get his hands on him, he caught a bit of his reflection in Mr. Doogan's broken computer screen.

"I'm naked!" he cried, leaping behind what was once the principal's desk. "Wait! I've never worn clothes, never wanted to either. *Zzzack!* It must be the glitch! That stupid wormhole fried my—"

He never finished his sentence. Lincoln picked up a chair leg and cracked him on the back of his head. Circuits popped and the robot fell face-first to the floor.

⚡

"Strange clothes," the bug leader said as he studied Finn. "And its face—I've never seen anything so ugly. What planet are you from?"

Finn stammered. The bug was so big, and walking and talking and carrying what looked like a weapon from one of his video games.

"He's another pathetic troublemaker, Major Kraven," one of the other bugs said. "Allow me the honor of killing him."

"No, me!" another bug cried.

"We're not killing either one of them. They can lead us to the weapon," Kraven said.

"Either one of them?" Finn asked.

"You and your partner, fool!"

"I don't have a partner."

"That would be me," a voice said from behind him. When Finn turned, he saw a girl was lying on the ground next to a dumpster. Her skin was the color of the sky and her hair was as orange as a bonfire. She seemed to be around his age, though the giant talking bugs didn't seem to bother her. In fact, she looked almost pleased with what was happening, like this was all a game. "Did Highbeam make it to the other side?"

"Huh?"

Kraven grabbed him roughly by the shoulders.

"You criminals are wasting your time and mine. You cannot save this foul-smelling planet, or any of the others. My people cannot be stopped. It is time to accept your fate. Hand over our weapon, or I will kill you where you stand," he hissed as his claw flipped a switch on his weapon. Finn heard a motor hum to life inside.

"I don't know anything about a weapon. I swear," Finn cried. "I didn't steal anything. I don't know her, either. I don't even know how I got here. I just want to go home!"

Another epic toilet flush filled his ears, and he felt his left hand jerk as if something was tugging on it. When he looked down, he realized he was still holding Kate's lunchbox, and it was bouncing around like it was full of overexcited frogs. The lid unzipped like before and a new wormhole appeared. It grew at a startling speed, and before he knew it, he was pulled inside. He was grateful to have left the bugs, but the trip was just as terrifying as the first. He screamed until he was spit out on the principal's office floor.

Lincoln was waiting for him. "Dude! What happened?"

Finn threw the lunchbox at him. Hard. He didn't know how to explain what just happened to him— blue girls, armed grasshoppers, trips through the galaxy . . . WAIT! Suddenly none of it mattered. He was smack in the middle of an even bigger problem.

"What did you do to Doogan's office?" he shouted as he gawked at the destruction.

"Don't blame me. It was him!" Lincoln pointed to the robot lying on the floor. "Don't worry. He's dead. You're welcome."

"We've got to clean this up," Finn said, panicking. He scooped up a stapler from the floor and went to set it on the desk but the desk was a pile of splinters.

"Are you kidding? We can't fix this!" Lincoln howled with laughter. "We're in a lot of trouble."

Trouble? That was the understatement of the century. When Doogan saw this mess, all those throbbing veins on his forehead would explode at the same time. It wasn't fair. He tried so hard. He kept his head down. He did what he was supposed to do.

This is Lincoln's fault! he raged. *If the big dumb jerk hadn't bullied me, none of this would have happened. I wouldn't have been sent to Mr. Doogan's office. I wouldn't have even opened my sister's lunchbox. I wouldn't have a library of weird space facts crowding my brain.*

Nothing Finn did or said would fix any of this. The only thing that made sense to him was to run.

"Derp!" Lincoln shouted. "Where are you going?"

Finn barreled into the hall and blasted out the emergency exit door with the alarm wailing in his ears. His sneakers hit the grass, and he sprinted through a crowd of dumbfounded kids.

He was so angry he could barely see where he was going, which explains why he crashed headfirst into someone. The impact sent them both bouncing to the ground.

"Finn Foley! Are you crazy?" a voice cried.

Finn sat up and rubbed his eyes, realizing he had accidentally clobbered Julep Li. Normally he would have helped her stand, but he was juggling two very important facts that demanded his attention: One— he'd nearly killed the coolest girl in school. Two—*Julep Li knew his name!*

Lincoln caught up to them, huffing and puffing. Before he could say anything, Julep was on her feet, poking her finger into his chest.

"Lincoln Sidana! Are you pickin' on him again?" she demanded.

Finn's heart cracked in half as a third fact pushed the first two aside: Julep Li knew Finn was Lincoln's punching bag. He was so humiliated. He wished another hole would open up and swallow him. He would jump in willingly.

"Huh?" Lincoln protested between heavy breaths. "I'm not picking on him. We were just attacked."

"Attacked?" Julep repeated.

"Yeah. By a robot."

Anger took over Finn. He did something he promised he would never do again. He clenched his fist and let it fly like a bolt of lightning. It hit Lincoln in his left eye, and the bully fell over like a tree. There was a collective gasp from the kids gathered on the lawn. Even Julep was stunned.

"Stay away from me, Lincoln," Finn said as he pushed his way through the crowd. "And stop calling me a derp!"

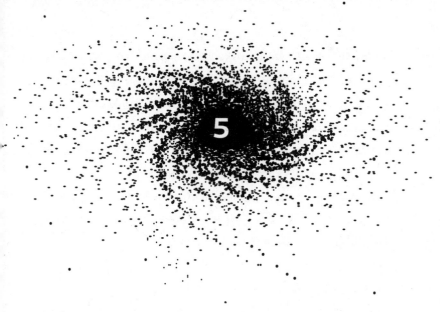

5

Mr. Doogan was having an awesome day. He helped the cafeteria workers find six missing bags of frozen peas. He stopped a fistfight between the math teacher and the librarian over a parking space. He ushered Darius Little into the bathroom before he barfed all over the hallway. Like his coffee mug said, he was the world's greatest principal. The icing on the cake would be the brand-new friendship of Finn Foley and Lincoln Sidana. Once they had some time to talk, he was sure they would see how much they had in common. Both were new to the school. Both had single parents. Both were smart. He could barely contain his excitement when he turned the knob of his office door to check on them.

The next thing he knew, he heard screaming. After

several moments he realized the screaming was coming out of him. His office was in shambles. His beautiful oak desk looked like it was karate-chopped in half by a giant. There were huge holes in the walls, his chair was a pile of toothpicks, and all that was left of his coffee mug was the handle. What had happened in the few short hours he left Finn and Lincoln alone? Where were they now? And why was there a pair of tighty-whities on the floor?

Before he could call for Ms. Applebaum, a hand clamped over his mouth.

"Shhh!"

Principal Doogan turned, but what he saw behind him didn't make any sense.

"Stay cool, partner. I'm not gonna hurt you. I just need to borrow some *zzzeeeck* clothes."

When Finn got home, he was all alone. Kate was still at school, and Mom was at work. The house was quiet and lonely, and he was thankful. It would give him time to think. He lay on the couch and stared at the water stain on the ceiling, dumbfounded at how quickly his life had been ruined. He was going to break his mom's heart, and there didn't seem to be a way to prevent it. He couldn't think of a thing he could say that would explain what happened at school. She'd never believe the truth. Who would?

So he did what he always did when he was stressed out: he fixed things. Helping around the house calmed him down and seemed to make things better for everyone. There were a million things in the house that needed fixing, too: the leaky sink, the busted garbage disposal, the broken screen door . . . the list went on and on.

He cleaned out the gutters on the back of the house, fixed the crooked downspout, sharpened the lawn mower blade, took apart the vacuum cleaner to find out why it was losing suction, and touched up the paint on the banister. If he didn't know how to do something, he watched a video about it online.

Hours passed. When he looked up at the clock, he realized Kate and Mom would be home soon, so he put all the tools away and went upstairs to the bathroom to wash his face. As the water ran down the drain, he stared at his reflection in the mirror. The boy looking back at him was tired and sad. He needed a haircut. His right hand was swollen from punching Lincoln in the eye. He barely recognized himself.

"What are we going to do?" he asked the reflection, but it offered no answers. There was, however, something odd poking out of his shirt, something that didn't belong.

He pulled off his sweatshirt and found a strange object on his chest. It was about the size of a birthday card and made from something thick and see-through. One side had a jagged edge, as if it was part of a bigger piece, and buried inside it were blinking lights. He touched its surface and watched them zip around.

"What are you?" he asked, but he already had his suspicions. Something hit him when he tried to close the lunchbox, something that came out of the whirlpool. Could it be the reason for his trip into space? If it was, he knew it had to go before it happened again. With frenzied fingers he tried to peel it off his skin, but it was stuck tight. When he tugged harder, it gave him a painful shock.

"Ouch!"

The zap wasn't the worst of it. When he looked around, he realized he was no longer in his bathroom. He was in the garage!

Snatching a pair of pliers off a table, he gripped a jagged corner of the object. *Zap!* Another painful sting and the scenery changed again. Now he was in the basement.

Finn fumbled for the light and found he was standing next to the washer and dryer. A bottle of liquid detergent sat on a shelf. Maybe it could help. He poured some onto his chest, soaking the strange machine in

the slippery soap, but when he gave it another pull—
zap! Now he was on the roof.

Without a ladder he was trapped up there, and
though it made him sick, he realized he had to poke the
machine on purpose just to get down. He only hoped he
didn't end up in the middle of a busy expressway. He
took a deep breath, braced himself for the shock, said
a little prayer, then yanked. He felt electricity rattle
his teeth, and suddenly he slammed against the bathroom wall and tumbled into the bathtub. A jarring pain
blasted his skull, and everything went black.

Kate was standing over him when he opened his eyes.
Her sandy blond hair was tied into a ponytail, and she
was wearing her full unicorn outfit, complete with the
tights, a sparkly sweater, and a hoodie with a purple
mane all the way down her back. A floppy golden horn
stuck out of the top of her head to complete the look.

"Why are you so weird?" she demanded.

He was too dazed to answer her. He wasn't even
sure where he was.

"Why are you home?" she continued. "Are you sick?
What's this thing on your chest?"

She reached out to touch it, but he squirmed away,
worried she'd get a *zap* and find herself floating in the
Hudson River.

"It's a science fair project," he lied.

She studied him up and down, but didn't challenge him.

"BTW—"

"BTW?"

"By. The. Way," she explained. "You put your ugly lunchbox in my backpack this morning. Everyone saw it. Do you have any idea how embarrassed I was?"

"I kinda do," he said. Lincoln's laughter was still echoing in his ears.

"Why aren't you at school?"

He lowered his eyes.

"OMG! Are you serious? What did you do?" she shouted.

"It's not my fault."

"Is this about Dad? You promised to stop getting in trouble! You told Mom you were over this!"

"I know!" he cried. "And I tried, but there's this kid—"

She waved her hands in the air as if his words were mosquitoes.

"Fix it!" she said as she stomped out of the room. "And I want my lunchbox back."

Finn climbed out of the tub and found his shirt in a ball on the floor. Before he pulled it back over his head, he gave the weird machine on his chest one last look. Sometimes it sent him into space; other times it dumped him in the bathtub. It didn't make sense. All he knew for certain was he didn't want anything to do with it.

~~~

Mom was a couple of hours late, which wasn't unusual, but on that day Finn expected her to come charging into the house, roaring at him like a lion. Instead, she set a pizza box on the kitchen table and fell into a chair.

"Today was the longest day of my life," she said. Her eyes looked tired. "Tell me something good."

Finn eyed her closely, wondering if this was some kind of trap, but when she smiled he realized she didn't have a clue about his day. Obviously Mr. Doogan hadn't called her, which in some ways made him feel worse. Now every time the phone rang he would have a heart attack. Maybe it was best to blurt it out. At least it would be over and he'd get a chance to tell his side of the story before Doogan told it for him. He was mustering the strength to spill the beans when Kate barged into the room.

"Pizza!" she cried, and did a happy dance . . . until she opened the lid and stepped back in horror. "Pine-apple and ham? Are you serious?"

"It's Finn's favorite," Mom reminded her. "We got your extra cheese and extra sauce last time."

"Extra cheese and extra sauce make sense! Fruit shouldn't be anywhere near a pizza. It's just wrong."

"You'll survive," Mom said. "So, anything interesting happen today?"

"Not for me," Kate said, then turned to Finn. "I went to school and followed all the rules. How about you, big brother? Is that what you did?"

Finn shot her an angry look. He still didn't know what to tell his mom, but rather than lie, he stuffed a slice into his mouth.

"How was your day?" he asked as he chewed.

"Just the same boring grown-up stuff I do every day," she said. "Sometimes I wish I was back in school like you two."

The doorbell rang and Finn yelped. Mr. Doogan was probably on the porch, with the police and any active-duty military he could find.

My life is over, he thought.

"I'll get it," Kate said.

"No! I'll get it," he shouted as he pushed past her.

When he got to the door, he was sure a couple of bites of pizza were on their way back up his throat. He started to sweat and felt a wobble in his knees. This was it. He closed his eyes, braced himself for the worst, and opened the door.

Mr. Doogan wasn't on the other side.

"Lincoln?"

"We've got a problem, derp," Lincoln said as he stepped into the light. Standing behind him was the robot, with a huge metal hand clamped on the back of Lincoln's neck, and an expression that told Finn he meant business.

"Where's the *zzzeeeck* gizmo, kid?"

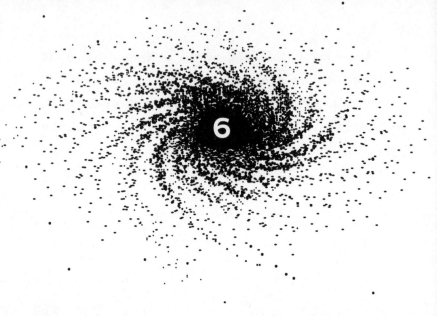

6

Finn stepped onto the porch and closed the door behind him. Without a word he ushered Lincoln and the robot into the garage, praying the neighbors wouldn't spot them through a window. Once inside, he flipped on the light. Lincoln's eye was purple and swollen. He couldn't help but feel a little proud. Now that the kid brought the robot to his house, he was tempted to hit him in the other eye.

"Why did you bring this thing to my house?" he said, pointing at the robot.

"'Thing'?" the robot interrupted. "Let's get something straight, Earth boy. The name's Highbeam, and I'm a Class-One Demo-Bot with a full upgrade package!"

"You're also seven feet tall and sound like a car crash when you walk. What if someone saw you? My neighbors are old. Ms. Pressman is almost one hundred! You could scare her to death."

"Trust me, kid. Coming to this dump of a planet wasn't my idea."

"And coming to your dump of a house wasn't mine," Lincoln said. "He yanked me through my bedroom window and forced me to bring him here."

"How did you know where I live?" Finn asked.

"Your world's information system . . . the internet. It gave me your address," Highbeam explained. "Interesting technology. So glad to see it's used for pictures of cats and complaining about movies. Anyway, I can't stand here flapping lips with you all night. Hand over the *zzzack* machine."

"Machine?" Finn asked.

"He hasn't stopped talking about it. Something called a butt generator," Lincoln explained.

"I told you it's called a wormhole generator fifteen times!" the robot corrected him.

Lincoln smirked, then turned to Finn. "I told him you wouldn't know what he was talking about."

"Actually, I think I do." Finn lifted his shirt, revealing the weird device glued to his chest.

"Dude!" Lincoln marveled at the circuits and lights. "What is that?"

Finn shrugged. "It flew out of the lunchbox and now it's stuck on me."

"Where's the rest of it?" the robot asked.

"Huh?"

"There's a piece missing," Highbeam said. "If you *zzzack* broke it, I'm gonna—"

"Finn?" Mom's voice drifted into the garage from outside. "The pizza is getting cold."

"I'll be right there!" he shouted.

"Who's that?" the robot demanded. "Can we trust her? Does she need to be captured?"

"She's my mom!" Finn said. He blinked at the robot. "Wait. Why are you wearing Mr. Doogan's clothes?"

"Oh, this is hilarious. Tell him, Buckethead," Lincoln said.

"I'm having some problems with my logic center," Highbeam said as his face turned a shade of pink. "It's made me *zzzeeeck* glitchy, and I'm having feelings I don't usually have, like not wanting to be naked."

"That doesn't answer my question. How did you get them from Mr. Doogan?"

The robot shuffled his feet and looked at the floor.

"I shocked his brain and stole them," he whispered.

"You did *what* to his brain?!"

"He'll be fine. The only side effects are some memory loss and an explosive bathroom visit."

Lincoln laughed so hard he could barely breathe.

"You think this is funny?"

"Kinda," Lincoln cried.

"Take this thing," Finn said to the robot as he gestured to his chest. "I want it off me. I want to forget this ever happened."

"I feel the same way, kid," Highbeam said, and before Finn could stop him, the robot grabbed the side of the device and pulled.

Zap! The robot's head spun around. Like before, Finn was transported. This time he landed in a broken-down tree house across the street. He climbed down the rickety ladder and ran back to the garage. When he got there, Lincoln and the robot stared at him in wonder.

"That was sick!" Lincoln said, looking impressed. "Do it again."

"This isn't a game!" Finn complained.

"Finn! Where are you?"

"Mommy's calling," Lincoln mocked.

"I need to go talk to her," Finn said. "Stay here and keep quiet, both of you."

"Okay, but be careful about what comes out of your yap," the robot said. "The fewer people who know about the gizmo and me, the better. I don't want to have to shock your mom's brain, too."

"No one is shocking my mom's brain!" Finn pulled his shirt down and went out into the yard. Mom was waiting on the front porch looking suspicious.

"What's going on? Who was at the door? I heard voices. Why are you hiding in the garage?" she pressed.

"I'm—"

Before Finn could come up with a lie, Lincoln appeared.

"Hey."

"I told you to stay in the garage," Finn muttered.

"You're not the boss of me," Lincoln replied.

"Well, hi!" Mom said as her face brightened. "Finn, why didn't you tell me you had a friend over?"

"'Cause I don't. We're not friends," Finn said.

"I'm Lincoln. I came to show Finn a robot," Lincoln said.

"Sounds fun! We've got pizza. Pineapple and ham. Would you like to come in for a slice?"

"He can't stay," Finn said.

"Maybe next time," Mom said. "All right, Finn. Don't stay out here too long."

After she went back inside, Finn pushed Lincoln into the garage and slammed the door.

"Is there something wrong with your brain?" he cried.

"You're the guy eating pineapple pizza," he said.

"Everything's a joke to you. Do you know what will happen if someone learns we're hiding a robot from outer space?"

"I actually don't," Lincoln said. "Tell me."

"Terrible stuff! Are you really that stupid?"

Wham! Finn found himself on the floor. His right

eye was aching. Lincoln stood over him with his fist clenched tight.

"Don't call me stupid," he growled, then stormed out of the garage, slamming the door behind him.

"You two have a weird friendship," Highbeam said.

"I hate that kid," Finn fumed. "Maybe more than I hate the stupid lunchbox."

"Lunchbox? What's a lunchbox?" the robot asked.

"Kids put sandwiches and bananas in them to eat at school. But this one has a hole that barfs up robots and shoots me into outer space," Finn grumbled.

A compartment opened on Highbeam's chest, and from inside he removed the familiar pink, sparkly unicorn lunchbox. "Is this what you're jabbering about? You left it behind."

"Keep that thing away from me," Finn said, taking a step back. "The last time I touched it I went to Nemeth and saw some giant bugs and a blue girl and—"

Highbeam grabbed him by the shoulders and lifted him off the ground so they were face to face.

"A blue girl. You saw Dax! She's alive! I can't believe it, kid. Listen, the gizmo on your chest is only half the size of the original machine. I think the other half is inside this lunchbox."

"So?"

"So, when we put them together, you become a super-advanced alien technology!"

"No! That's terrible."

"Really terrible, 'cause if it's true, you are wanted by an evil empire of hungry space bugs. But there is good news. You can take me home! I'm sure there's someone back there who can help get it off your chest. The Resistance has a lot of bug brains working for it. Fire it up. Let's go!"

"Forget it! I'm not touching that lunchbox ever again. The last time I did, a bunch of monsters tried to kill me. If your friends want this machine, they are going to have to come here and get it themselves."

"Then I've got some bad news for you, Earth boy. At sub–light speed, it will take my friends a hundred thousand years to come here and pick me up."

"A hundred thousand years?" Finn cried.

"Yep, and that's if no one stops for a bathroom break."

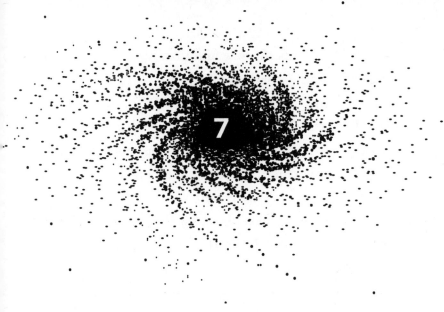

7

Principal Doogan woke up on the floor. He wasn't sure how he got there. His memory was like a block of Swiss cheese—milky and full of holes. He also didn't know why his office looked like a war zone, or what happened to his clothes. All he had on were boxer shorts and black socks.

He felt wobbly getting to his feet, and the back of his head hurt something fierce. Once upright, he glanced at the wall for the clock, but it was broken and lying on the floor. The moon outside the window was his only clue to the time. It was late. He must have been out for hours.

He wondered if he should call the police, but he had no idea how to explain everything to them. It wouldn't end well, for sure. It was best to go home and get some rest. Maybe his memory would give up some answers in the morning.

Unfortunately, Old Pete was in the hallway, dragging a floor buffer behind him. The custodian was pushing eighty-five. He spent most days yammering about how much things used to cost when he was a boy, and how kids today didn't appreciate a good story about how much things used to cost. He was slow, too, slower than the last day of school. It took him three times as long to do even the simplest chore. Doogan wondered why he didn't retire, but Old Pete said the job kept him young. Now Doogan wished he had insisted.

Doogan watched patiently as the floor buffer got away from Old Pete a few times, and nearly killed him twice, but eventually the floors were finished. It wasn't a moment too soon. Mr. Doogan's belly was churning and sour. He was dripping with sweat. He needed to find a toilet fast. He darted from his office to the boys' bathroom. Everything was smaller in there, but his stomach wasn't giving him a choice. It was the most explosive event of his life on the tiniest toilet he had ever used.

When his suffering was over, he checked the halls for Old Pete, then dashed toward the exit. Before he pushed the door open, he stopped in his tracks. He didn't have his car keys. They were in his pants pocket, and his pants were missing.

Walking home was his only option, though he doubted he'd get very far. People would notice a nearly naked man jogging down the highway. He had to find something to wear. Wait! The lost-and-found box outside Ms. Applebaum's office was usually overflowing with clothes. The vice principal loved showing him what she found inside it—a full-length evening gown, snorkeling flippers, a wooden leg. Maybe he would get lucky and find a pair of pants and a shirt.

The freshly waxed floors were like a slip and slide as he made his way toward Ms. Applebaum's office. The box was exactly where she kept it, but it was empty except for a rainbow-colored clown wig, a pair of sweatpants for a seven-year-old, and a plastic sword. The school must have donated the unclaimed stuff to charity when the box got full.

He was out of options. His career was over. Who would hire him when this story came out? *Naked Principal Banned from Teaching!* He would be a laughingstock.

He had no choice but to ask Old Pete for help. On his way to find him, he noticed a photo hanging on Ms. Applebaum's wall. It was taken at a pep rally a few years ago. He stood in the center of the gym, cheering into a megaphone as excited students applauded. Next to him was the school's mascot—Roger the Fighting Raccoon. It was Roger's last pep rally. Mr. Griffin, who wore the costume, complained it was full of bed bugs. He refused to wear it again, and poor Roger was stuffed in a closet in the music room and forgotten.

Until now!

Minutes later Mr. Doogan zipped himself into the furry black-and-white suit. It was hot and heavy and Roger's feet were huge, making it difficult to walk. Plus, Mr. Griffin wasn't exaggerating about the bed bugs. The principal could feel them feasting on his skin already. Still, it was better than walking home in his undies. Leaving Roger's bulky head behind, he stomped through the exit door into the cool night air and pointed himself toward home.

The best way to avoid attention was to scurry through backyards, but he regretted it immediately. An old woman turned her garden hose on him. A pack of cats attacked him from out of nowhere. But the biggest humiliation was walking past the window of a young girl. He expected her to scream, but instead, she snatched her phone and took pictures of him. He recognized her from school.

Her name was Julep Li.

Meanwhile, Old Pete was back at school getting ready to give Mr. Doogan's office a good mopping. He wheeled his bucket down the hall and opened the principal's door. A moment later he had the sheriff's department on the phone.

"Hello, Deputy," he said. "I'm calling from the elementary school. I want to report a kidnapping."

"I can't take you in my house," Finn cried.

"Listen, kid. I was sent here to guard the gizmo," Highbeam explained. "The fate of the universe and everyone in it depends on me *zzzack* keeping it out of the wrong hands, and buster, you definitely have the wrong hands. So, as long as it's stuck on you, so am I. And before you get any clever ideas like locking me out, just know you'll have a robot-sized hole in the side of your *zzzack* house if you try."

Finn threw up his hands. "Fine! But stay out of sight and be quiet."

A zipper appeared on the robot's face and pulled itself closed.

Finn tiptoed out of the garage with the robot at his heels. Highbeam's metallic body was loud, and his weight caused each porch step to cry out for mercy. Finn opened the front door and poked his head inside, and when he didn't see anyone, he gestured for Highbeam to follow.

The robot smacked his head on the doorframe. *THUMP!* The impact nearly knocked a lamp over.

"Finn?"

Finn shoved Highbeam toward the stairs and the robot sprang up them just as Mom rounded the corner.

"He seems nice," Mom said.

"Huh?"

"That boy, Lincoln. I'm glad you're making friends."

Finn was too distracted to correct her.

"Oh, honey. What happened to your eye?" she asked. When she ran her thumb across his cheek, it stung.

"It's nothing. I walked into a door," he lied. He'd almost forgotten about Lincoln's sucker punch.

"You have to be more careful. Put some ice on it or you'll look like you've been in a fight," she said as she wrapped him in a hug.

"What was that for?" he asked.

"Can't a mom give her kid a hug? Finn, I know this hasn't been an easy year. It started out bumpy but I can see you're trying. It means a lot to me."

"You're welcome," he said, though he felt like a con artist.

Highbeam wasn't waiting when Finn got upstairs. In a panic, Finn charged into Kate's room, expecting a scream of terror as Highbeam towered over her. Instead, she was dancing on her bed and singing into a hairbrush.

"Unicorns have power greater than you know.
Come along and watch our magic grow!
Whip your mane, blow a kiss to the wind,
Unicorn Magic will always win!"

When Kate saw him, she stuck out her tongue.

"Seriously? Don't you know how to knock? Go away! I'm watching *Unicorn Magic*," she said as she gestured to the show streaming on her computer. "Tonight we find out which unicorn is Proudheart's long-lost sister. I've waited all year for this, and I'm not going to let you ruin it."

"Sorry," he said. "I was just . . . worried about you."

She paused for a second, eyeing him curiously. "Oh. Do—do you want to watch it with me?"

"I do, but—"

"Forget it. You never want to do anything with me," she grumbled. He knew she was hurt, and worse, she was right. He had been a jerk for months, sulking in his room, avoiding everyone, and despite it all she still wanted him around. It was another thing to feel bad about, but there was a missing seven-foot-tall robot in the house that had to come first.

He breathed a sigh of relief when he found the bathroom and Mom's room were robot-free. There was only one more place to look—his bedroom. He found

Highbeam there, lying on his bed, and flipping through a comic book.

"This is ridiculous. There is no planet called Krypton. Sure, the children on Somoza can fly until they hit puberty, but heat vision? That's just silly." He tossed the comic aside and sprang to his feet, tearing the back of Mr. Doogan's pants in the process. His faceplate turned bright red. "Fudge. You got anything else I can wear around here?"

"You know, zapping someone's brain and then stealing their clothes is rude," Finn said. "Maybe you should be more careful."

"Kid, the people on this planet are tiny. *Zzzack!* I'm doing the best I can."

Finn asked him to wait, then went to his mom's room. Her closets were full of dresses and skirts. Highbeam might not want to wear them, but then again, beggars can't be choosers. He was about to take a polka-dot dress when he noticed some boxes crammed in the back corner. When he knelt down and opened one, he discovered it was full of his dad's old clothes.

A cowboy hat was on top. Finn had never seen it before and couldn't imagine his dad ever wearing one. He set it aside. Underneath was something he definitely recognized—an Ohio State University sweatshirt. His dad wore it all the time. When Finn buried his nose in it, he could still smell his father's scent in the fabric. It brought back memories of ice fishing at the lake, lazy afternoons on the couch, watching him shave in the bathroom mirror, hearing the racket he'd make in the kitchen trying to surprise everyone with pancakes. Those were happy days and his heart ached for them, but he pushed the memories away. He promised himself he would never let his dad make him sad again.

In another box, he found a Hawaiian shirt and a pair of jeans splattered with paint. There was a brown suit jacket and a red necktie Finn gave his dad on Father's Day. Highbeam would ruin them for sure, but that was fine. Let him rip them to shreds!

Once he was back in his room, Finn watched Highbeam squeeze into the odd outfit, then spin around in the mirror like a fashion model.

"Looking good, looking good! *Zzzzzack!*" the robot said. "Stupid glitch! Dax would think this was hilarious."

"Your partner?"

"We joined the Resistance on the same day, and we've been working together ever since. We were assigned to the Plague mothership to watch and report back what we found, but then we stumbled on the gizmo and everything went sideways."

"The Plague? You mean the grasshopper people with the big guns?"

"They're actually giant locusts, and the greatest threat the universe has ever seen. They invade planets and eat up all the resources until the environment collapses, then they move on. Nemeth used to be a paradise, but now—well, it won't be long before it's a ball of dust. The Resistance has to find a way to stop them before it's too late. The gizmo could be the answer to a lot of prayers."

Finn lifted his shirt to look at the strange machine on his chest.

"So, this could save your world?"

"It could save the entire universe," Highbeam said.

"There has to be another way to get it off of me," Finn said. "You're a robot. Don't you have a big computer for a brain? You can figure this out, right?"

Highbeam shrugged. "I'm a Demo-Bot, or I was before I became a spy. I'm designed to knock buildings down. I don't have a lot of experience removing advanced *zzzack* technologies from the bodies of whiney Earth kids."

Finn frowned and kicked off his shoes, suddenly feeling the day catching up to him. He was too tired to even get undressed. He crawled into bed and pulled the covers up to his chin.

"I have to go to sleep," he said as he reached over and flipped off the lamp.

The dim light of Highbeam's face painted the room in a golden glow.

"How long do Earth kids sleep?"

"Usually eight hours, maybe nine."

"Nine hours! That's so lazy! No wonder this planet hasn't invented *zzzeeeck* interstellar travel yet. I guess I could give myself a hard restart. It might fix this *zzzack* glitch, but I'll be completely off-line for a while. Are there any dangers on this planet I need to know about?"

"Like what?"

"Four-Winged Creeper Droids?"

"I don't know what that is."

"Slervian Slime Eaters?"

Finn shook his head.

"Prickly Hand Apes? Invisible Phantom Ghouls? Man-Eating Asparagus Stalks?"

"You made that last one up, didn't you?"

The robot chuckled. He removed the lunchbox from his chest compartment and set it next to Finn's bedside lamp.

"You gotta keep an eye on this while I'm off-line," Highbeam said.

"Trust me, no one is going to steal that ugly thing," Finn said.

He watched the robot rise to his full height as he prepared to power down. He couldn't tell what was weirder—a robot in his bedroom or a robot wearing his dad's old clothes.

"Do robots have dads?" he asked.

Highbeam nodded. "Sure."

"How does that work?"

"You're going to have to ask your mom about the transistors and the plasma cuffs," Highbeam said. "But yes, robots have kids. I have twenty-five."

"Twenty-five! That's a lot of kids. They must miss you."

Highbeam nodded.

"I miss them, too, but they know I will always come home to them. This time it's just going to take longer than normal. They're with my ex. It's . . . complicated."

A hundred thousand years, Finn thought. He glanced at the lunchbox and couldn't help but feel guilty. It wasn't right to keep Highbeam from his kids if he had the power to send him home. Even if flying through space was scary, he was being selfish.

"Listen, I'll take you home in the morning," he promised.

"Really? Aw, that's great, kid! I'm going to delete all the terrible things I was thinking about you from my memory chips."

"I just really need to sleep."

"Sure. You do that. Sleep tight. Don't let the Brocklian Sand Mites eat your brain," the robot said.

"Huh?"

"It's something we tell children at bedtime on Nemeth."

"And that helps them sleep?"

Highbeam shrugged. His motors whirred down and his digital face faded to black until he was nothing more than a silhouette in the moonlight. Finn's dad used to stand over his bed until he fell asleep and the memory made him sad. He tried to force it out of his mind, but this one was too stubborn. He envied Highbeam. He wished he could erase thoughts from his head, too.

8

Kate tossed and turned. The new *Unicorn Magic* episode was epic, and her brain replayed every shocking twist. Nightdancer was Proudheart's sister! Nightdancer! Seriously! All Kate's friends were wrong. Alba was positive it was Brighteyes, and Lucia guessed it was Truespirit. Even Georgia, who'd binged six seasons in one weekend and knew every line of dialog, was surprised. Of course, a member of the Shadow Herd was always a possibility, but Nightdancer? She and Proudheart were complete opposites. This would change everything! In fact, nothing in Prancer Meadows would ever be the same!

And now the show was making everyone wait a week for a new episode! Kate couldn't wait a week! There was too much unicorn drama. Would Tailwind ever find the enchanted gem? Would Sunbeam finally see that June-berry was just trying to be a good friend? Would Princess Rainstorm stand up to her controlling uncle, King Snowcap, and learn to use her weather powers?

Kate could hardly stand it!

Overwhelmed by unicorn joy, she rushed to her dresser to gaze at her collection of unicorn figurines. Something was missing. Her lunchbox! Finn never gave it back to her, and knowing him, it was probably buried under a mountain of his stinky stuff. She needed to rescue it before he ruined it with his funk.

She crept through the dark hallway to his room and spotted it on his nightstand. Its glitter shimmered in the moonlight. She was so focused on getting it back she missed the enormous, seven-foot metallic robot standing over her brother's bed.

Back in her room, Kate set the lunchbox in its proper place among her *Unicorn Magic* dolls and crawled back into bed, ready to dream of Prancer Meadow.

A noise startled her. It sounded like a toilet flush, only it was really, really loud.

Kate sat up. Her lunchbox was hopping up and down like there was something inside it trying to get out.

⚡

Finn woke to what sounded like a tiny drum solo under his blanket. He yanked up his sweatshirt. The machine was as bright as a Christmas tree. What was wrong with it? What if it caught fire or exploded?

"Uh . . . Highbeam," he said to the robot. "Something is happening."

Highbeam's face was dark. He was still powered down. Finn knocked on his head, but it didn't wake him up. Now the machine was rattling. Maybe he was too close to the lunchbox, but when he looked to his bedside table, he discovered it was missing. Someone had taken it, but who? And why?

And that was when he heard Kate scream. Finn dashed into her room. She was wearing her unicorn hoodie and waving a tennis racket at the lunchbox. It was hovering above her bed and the zipper was opening.

"What did you do to my lunchbox?" she croaked.

"Get down! Now!"

Finn yanked Kate to the floor just as the lid popped open. Bolts of electricity filled the room. A whirlpool of stars appeared and he braced himself to be sucked inside it—but this time something was different.

This time something came out.

It started with a spindly leg, followed by another, and another. Soon, a six-foot-tall locust stood in his room, with a long tail, flapping wings, and huge, empty eyes. Its body was yellow, but Finn recognized the red markings on its face. It was Sin Kraven, the same bug that threatened to kill him on Nemeth! But something was off about him. The monster looked sick and blind. He stumbled on its many feet, banging around Kate's room, knocking things off shelves.

"Run!" Finn cried.

Together, they darted to Finn's room and locked the door tight, pressing their backs against it.

"What was that?" Kate cried.

"Remember this afternoon when you found me in the bathtub and I told you I was in trouble?" Finn asked. "That thing is part of it."

"What about that?" Kate said, gesturing to High-beam. "This is a bad dream, right? It's because of that stupid pineapple pizza!"

"It's not the pizza!" Finn said. "This is really happening. Just stay calm, and—"

A knock at the door caused them both to scream.

"What on earth is going on in there?" Mom cried from the other side. "It's four in the morning!"

Finn opened the door just wide enough for them to step out and quickly closed it behind them.

"Kate saw a bug," Finn said.

"All this screaming is about a bug?" Mom's hair stuck out in weird poofs on her head. She did not look amused.

"It was a big bug!" Kate whispered.

"Both of you are too old to have meltdowns about a

spider!" Before they could stop her she marched into Kate's bedroom.

"Mom! No!"

"Where is this huge bug threatening to kill you both?" Mom said as she searched around angrily. Kraven was gone. The only proof he had been there at all was Kate's open bedroom window and the enormous weapon on her floor. Kraven must have dropped it when he made his escape.

"What's this?" Mom said as she picked it up.

"My science fair project," Finn said as he snatched it away.

"Well, here's the problem," Mom said. She closed the window tight and locked it. "If you leave your window open all night, bugs are going to fly in here. Honestly, Kate, that's just common sense. Now everyone go back to bed!"

Mom stomped back to her room, promising to ground them both if they weren't asleep in ten minutes.

"Start talking, Finn!" Kate said the moment they were alone.

Finn led her back to his room.

They sat on the bed and he explained everything as best he could.

"Who else knows about this?" she asked.

"Lincoln Sidana."

"The jerk that keeps beating you up?"

"How do you know about that?"

"Everyone knows about it. I just don't know why you keep letting it happen," Kate said.

"I made Mom a promise," he said. "No more trouble."

Kate moved to the window and peered into the night.

"It took the lunchbox," she said. "That's not good, is it?"

Finn shook his head.

"I'm sleeping in here," she said, jumping into his bed and under his covers.

Finn didn't argue. She was scared. He propped the bug's massive weapon in the corner, then got into bed next to her. In the dark she found his hand. He gave it a squeeze, hoping to reassure her. She squeezed back.

"Why is the robot wearing Dad's clothes?" Kate whispered.

"He doesn't like to be naked," Finn said.

"Weird," she said. "Don't let him near my unicorn tights. He'll ruin them."

9

Mr. Doogan was miserable. The costume was as hot as a furnace. The tail dragged on the ground, collecting twigs and leaves, and the bedbugs were treating him like an all-you-can-eat buffet. Every couple of steps, he had to stop and scratch himself with his oversized raccoon paws.

The moon was the only thing on his side. It was full and bright and shined enough light to make his way. He stomped along the hiking trail he'd found and tried to remember his day. Images flashed in his mind like photographs—his demolished office, Finn Foley begging for another chance, bags of frozen peas, and the strangest thing of all—a robot. He knew it wasn't real, but it felt real, and it kept popping up. Each time it appeared, it brought a brain-punching headache and a gurgle in his belly.

He climbed to the top of a rise and stopped to lean against a tree, his heart racing and sweat pouring down his face. There he noticed a raccoon—a real one— watching him from the brush. It didn't seem afraid of him. Instead, it looked hypnotized, as if it were trying to understand what he was. After a moment or two, it scurried out of the bushes and got close enough to sniff Doogan's foot.

"Hey, little brother." Mr. Doogan chuckled. "I must look pretty strange to you. Well, don't worry. I'm just passing through."

The raccoon let loose with an angry bark.

"Whoa! Take it easy. I'm going. I'm going," Doogan promised.

The raccoon bared its fangs.

Doogan growled back at it.

The raccoon hissed.

Doogan did the same.

The raccoon lifted its leg and took a leak on Doogan's foot.

"Why, you dirty little fur ball!" he cried.

The insult seemed to offend the raccoon. It leaped onto the principal's chest, shrieking and clawing. Luckily, the mascot costume was made of thick fabric and protected him, but Mr. Doogan was still scared. He tried to swat the creature away, but the raccoon didn't back down. Desperate, he grabbed the critter by the tail and flung it into the woods. An angry howl filled the night, followed by the sound of furious feet fleeing the scene.

"Can't anything go right for me today?" Doogan asked.

"I feel the same way," a voice said from the shadows.

"Who's there?" Doogan said, spinning around.

A giant bug stepped out of the darkness. It had huge snapping mandibles and enormous wings. Mr. Doogan had never seen a bug so big, let alone one that could talk. It was wearing a strange jacket covered in medals and carrying a pink lunchbox.

"What planet is this?" it demanded.

Doogan stammered, too frightened to put words together.

"Where am I, fool?" the monster shouted.

"Earth!"

"Earth? I've never heard of it, but no mind. Take me to the place where you keep your hoppers!"

"I don't understand—"

"Your offspring! Where do you house them? A hopper from this planet has stolen the most powerful weapon in the universe, and I will get it back."

"What are you?" Doogan asked, horrified.

The bug seized him by the neck. It was incredibly strong. Doogan couldn't pull away.

"I will ask the questions! For now, I am not feeling well. My trip through the wormhole has weakened me. I need rest, but when I am strong again you will help me find the boy so I can kill him."

"What boy?" Doogan cried, but before he got an answer the bug's wings extended and they were both flying into the night sky.

Finn woke to Highbeam tapping him on the head with his heavy metal finger.

"Wake up, kid. I'm packed and ready to go," the robot said.

"Hey! Take it easy," Finn complained. "That's where I keep my brain."

"Who's this?" the robot said, scooping a still-sleeping Kate up into his huge hands. He turned her over and over as if she were a fancy vase.

"She's my sister."

Kate screamed until Highbeam clamped his hand over her mouth.

"She's loud," the robot said. "And squirmy. Hey, no biting!"

"She had a rough night. We both did. A locust came out of the lunchbox."

"What?" Highbeam asked.

"I think his name is Sin Kraven. He threatened to kill me on Nemeth."

"Why didn't you tell me?"

"I tried, but you wouldn't wake up!"

"You shouldn't have fooled around with the gizmo! It's dangerous."

"I didn't touch that thing!" Finn cried. "The lunch-box wasn't even in my room at the time."

"That doesn't make a lick of sense! How does it work if the two pieces aren't in contact?" Highbeam said. "So what did you do with Kraven?"

"Do with him? Nothing! We ran away," Kate explained, finally wrestling herself free.

"Ran away!" Highbeam was so mad, his digital face became a roaring fire.

"Seriously? It was a giant bug!" Kate cried.

"He jumped out her window," Finn said. "And I've got more bad news. He took the lunchbox with him."

"Did I forget to tell you the gizmo is a very danger-ous weapon and the fate of trillions of life-forms are dependent on keeping it away from the evil, planet-conquering empire of giant bugs? 'Cause I sorta re-member telling you that."

"Finn!" Mom knocked on the door. She tried the knob, but Finn had locked it. "Let me in."

"Hang on!" Finn said, then turned to the robot. "You have to hide."

Highbeam glanced around the room. A question mark appeared on his face.

"Can't you turn invisible or something? You know, like cloak mode?"

"I'm a robot. Not a wizard *zzzeeeck!* Oh, dag nabbit. The stupid glitch is back!"

Kate pulled the sheet off the bed and draped it over the robot's head.

"Oh, she'll never notice that," Finn said.

"I'm trying to help!" Kate said.

"Stay quiet." Finn unlocked the door. He squeezed into the hall, expecting Mom to be grouchy from the night before, but she had an odd smile on her face.

"Oh, honey. Your eye looks so bruised," she said. "You should have put some ice on it."

"I forgot."

There was a loud thump in his room.

"What's going on in there?"

"Kate and I are . . . playing unicorns."

"Really?"

"Yep. I'm Twinkletoes, and she's Cornball, and we're having a dance party in the Rainbow Mountains."

Mom smiled. "I hate to break up the fun, but there's someone downstairs who wants to talk to you."

Doogan! In all the excitement, Finn totally forgot about the principal. He was finally here to ruin his life.

"Mom, I can't explain everything—"

"She says her name is Julep," Mom said.

"Julep? Julep Li . . . is downstairs?"

"Maybe you should change into some clean clothes. And brush your hair and teeth," she said.

"Why should I do all that?" he asked.

Mom smiled. "You can't play dumb with me, Finn. I'll keep her company. I bet she'd love to see all those old baby pictures of you in the bathtub."

"MOM!"

"I'm just teasing," Mom said as she went down the stairs. "Or am I?"

Back in his room, Kate and Highbeam waited. His sister had the same corny smile as his mother.

"Who's Julep?" she said. "Do you like her? Is she your girlfriend?"

"She's nobody. Just a girl from school."

"Who cares?" Highbeam said. "We have a crisis on our hands. We need to find Kraven and get the lunchbox back. Go get rid of her, lover boy."

"I'll find out what she wants and send her home," he said. Finn snatched a change of clothes and went to the bathroom. One look at his black eye and he burned with embarrassment. He brushed his teeth and combed his hair, fighting with a patch in the back that would not lie down.

"Who cares what you look like?" Highbeam cried, "We have work to do!"

Finn found Julep sitting on his front porch stoop. Her backpack was next to her and she was reading a book called *Our Coming Computer Overlords.*

"Be cool," he whispered to himself as he stepped outside.

"Good morning, Finn Foley," she said. "We've got a lot to talk about."

"We do?" he said.

"What's up, derp?" Lincoln stepped out from behind a bush. His eye was a deep purple. He was also wearing the same clothes as the night before.

"What are you doing here?" Finn asked.

"She wouldn't leave me alone until I brought her here," he complained. "It's starting to feel like a pattern."

"Tell me about the robot," Julep said.

"Robot?" Finn turned to Lincoln and flashed him an angry look. "Oh, you mean that thing Lincoln said yesterday? That was a big, dumb joke. Tell her it was a *joke,* Lincoln."

Julep frowned.

"All right, so that's how you're going to do this?

Fine. Yesterday the two of you came running out of the school angrier than a couple of wet cats. Lincoln said you were attacked by a robot. Today the police are outside the school. They say the principal's office has been demolished. He's missing," Julep said matter-of-factly. She handed Finn her phone. On the screen was a picture of a very startled Mr. Doogan wearing some kind of costume. "That's our principal creeping around my backyard last night dressed as a raccoon. That's three weird things. I'm an expert on weird things, and I've learned that if one part of a weird story is true, the rest of the story is probably true, too. So, Finn Foley, before another lie falls out of your mouth, why don't you show me the robot, because believe it or not, I'm here to help."

Finn looked at Lincoln, then back at Julep. There was no use lying to her.

"What do you know about bugs?" he asked.

Julep's eyebrows rose, and she smiled. "A lot."

He took Julep and Lincoln up to his room and stopped them at his door.

"Don't freak out," he told Julep. "If you freak out my mom will come up here and—"

"I'm not going to freak out," she promised.

Finn opened the door. Highbeam and Kate were waiting on the other side.

Julep slowly entered with Lincoln behind her.

Everyone watched as she circled Highbeam, peering at him from every angle. She sat down on Finn's bed, took his pillow, and stuffed it over her face. Then she screamed with delight.

"What is she doing?" Highbeam asked.

"Freaking out," Lincoln said.

"I KNEW IT!" The pillow muffled Julep's happy squeaks. "EVERYONE SAID I WAS CRAZY, BUT I KNEW IT!"

She put the pillow back where she found it.

"Feeling better?" Kate asked.

"Much. But I might have to do it again later."

10

"Quick question," Highbeam said as the group hiked along a forest trail. "Are we gonna tell everyone on this planet about me?"

"It's not my fault," Finn said as he gestured to Julep. She followed them while thumbing through a book on bugs. "She figured it out."

"I'm unusually clever," she said. Somehow it came out sounding less like a brag and more like a fact. "Hey, I found something. Locusts are loners. They stick to themselves, but in the right environment they can go into a frenzy and form a swarm. It's called a plague."

"We need to focus on where he might be hiding and how he got here in the first place," Highbeam said.

"He's right. How did Kraven get here? I thought you said the machine was one of a kind. Could the Plague build another one?" Finn asked.

"The guards Dax and I stole it from said its inventor died in prison. I guess the bugs could have a copy of the designs, but they're crazy complicated."

"Actually, I have a theory," Julep said as she pushed her glasses up the bridge of her nose. She took off her pack, shoved the bug book inside, and took out another. It was called *Alien Visitors—Space, Time, and Wormhole Theories*.

She flipped through the pages until she found what she wanted.

"Here it is. My guess is the bug came through a rift."

"A rift?" Kate repeated.

"Is this going to be a lot of science stuff?" Lincoln asked.

"Imagine the machine like it's a shovel. It digs a hole, not in the ground but in space. It basically makes a tunnel from one part of the universe to another, creating a shortcut between the two places and turning a trip that could take thousands of years into one that takes seconds. And just like a tunnel, you have to create an opening on one end and exit on the other. But this is why the machine is special. It closes both ends of the tunnel once you've used it." She paused. "At least

I think that's what it does. Since Highbeam and his partner threw the machine into the tunnel, it couldn't close one of the ends."

"So you think it's still open?" Highbeam said.

Julep nodded. "The opening is still there on your world, and the exit is inside the lunchbox. That's called a rift."

"Kraven must have found the entrance," Finn said.

"Um, I have a question," Kate said. "If the tunnel is still open on Nemeth, can't more bugs find their way here?"

"Yes," Julep said.

"How many more are there?" Lincoln asked Highbeam.

"Millions," he said. The robot stopped and scanned the forest. Down below was the little town of Cold Spring with its tiny two-story buildings, each with a thin trail of smoke drifting from its chimney. It was so quaint and unprepared. Finn knew what Highbeam was going to say before he said it.

"Kraven might be here for the gizmo, but he will notice how perfect this world is for the Plague. There is so much here to eat, enough for generations, and there's nothing to stop them. They could conquer this world in ten minutes."

"We have to find that bug," Julep said.

"And when we do, I need to get back home and warn the Resistance," Highbeam told Finn.

Once again, Finn felt guilty. He should have taken Highbeam home the night before, and now Kraven had half the generator.

"So why are we out here in the woods?" Lincoln said.

"Locusts are always hungry," Julep said. "They have to eat several times a day, and what they mostly eat is plants. A lot of the trees and grass down in the town are dying because winter is on the way, but up here, some of the trees stay green all year long."

"But wandering around is not getting us anywhere," Highbeam complained. A compartment opened in his chest. Inside was a gadget with a small screen and a meter. While he fiddled with the knobs, a needle on the screen bounced around.

"Is that some kind of laser gun?" Lincoln asked, his eyes wide with hope.

"Calm down, kid. It's a heartbeat detector," the robot explained. "It's one of the tools of the trade I used back when I made my living knocking down buildings on construction sites. Always a good idea to make sure a house is empty of people before you stomp through it. I've never used it on a big open space like this, but it's worth a try."

The meter let out a faint whine that grew louder when Highbeam pointed it deep into the woods.

"Something's over there," he said, pointing down the path.

"Could be an animal," Lincoln said.

"Could be a bigfoot!" Julep cried.

"Could be dangerous," Highbeam said as he put the meter away and pulled his hand cannon out of the built-in slot on his hip. "I think maybe the four of you should hang back and let me scout out the situation. Kraven is desperate, and that makes him deadly. Besides, some of us are not dressed for a fight."

Kate looked down at her unicorn pajamas. "Hey! Unicorns are awesome."

"You'll get no arguments from me, little lady. I've seen them in a fight firsthand."

Kate gasped.

Highbeam raced into the woods without another word and vanished among the trees.

"Unicorns are real?" Kate cried. "Seriously?"

"Well, I guess we just wait," Finn said.

Without warning, Julep stepped off the path and headed in the direction the robot went.

"Where are you going?" Finn called out.

"You're crazy if you think I'm going to miss seeing a real live alien," Julep said.

Lincoln shrugged. "She's got a point. Robot versus giant bug. I think I have to see that," he said, and chased after her.

"C'mon," Kate said, running after the group.

"Guys? Come back!" Finn cried, but when they didn't answer, he was forced to follow, too.

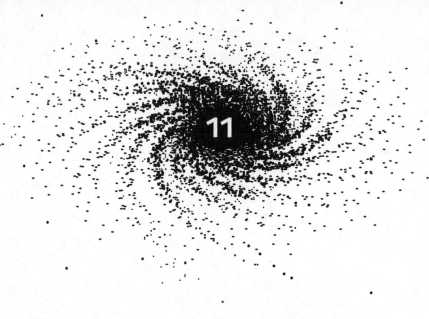

11

The worst part about being kidnapped by a giant flying insect were the crash landings. The bug—who called himself Major Sin Kraven—couldn't stay in the air. He was nauseous and weak. His eyesight was damaged from going through something he called a wormhole, and he slammed into trees, knocking both of them out of the air over and over again. Luckily, the Roger the Raccoon costume protected Mr. Doogan from serious injuries.

After the last crash, Kraven dragged himself into the bushes to throw up, leaving Doogan to wait on a dry, rocky hillside overlooking the river. *Think, Doogan! How do you get out of this?* he said to himself. *You are a professional educator. You're smart.*

Fighting the monster was the best of a lot of bad

options. Unfortunately, Kraven was strong, was nearly as tall as him, and had a body covered in a hard shell, like a suit of armor. It would take a surprise attack to hurt him. Mr. Doogan scanned the ground for a fallen branch or anything he could use as a weapon. There wasn't much to choose from, but he spotted something that would make a good club. Before he could get it, Kraven returned.

"The wormhole opened inside the boy's fortress," the bug said. "I was blind and sick and there was a loud, screeching creature with a horn on its head, so I did not get a good look. I had to use my scanner to escape. Luckily, I found this as I fled." He held out the lunchbox. "It's one half of the weapon I seek. No doubt the boy has hidden the rest. You will help me find his fortress again. Do your hoppers live with other warriors?"

"You mean, our children? Most of them stay with their families at—"

"Interesting. The parents train them for battle in the home," Kraven interrupted. "My people have found we need to separate the offspring from the rest of the brood or the siblings eat one another."

"Our families encourage the little ones to eat their brothers and sisters. It teaches them to be ruthless," Mr. Doogan lied. It dawned on him that the less information Kraven had about Earth, the better. "Survival of the fittest is how we do things. I, um, killed and ate two of my brothers just so I could have my own room."

"Indeed," Kraven said with a hint of respect.

"Yes, but surviving cannibalism doesn't guarantee your safety. Many of our warriors die during battle training, but what can you expect when gorillas are the instructors? And don't forget about the army of electric eels and tigers who teach them to fight in armed combat. Only one in a hundred children grow to be adults, but they're the meanest, toughest children you would ever want to run into. If I were you, I'd give up this plan. Any kid on this planet will rip off your arm and feed it to you before even saying hello!"

Kraven studied him closely. Doogan worried the bug could see through his lies.

"At what age does your kind grow your pelts?"

"Pelts?" Mr. Doogan looked down at himself and realized the monster believed his costume was his skin. "Around age twelve. If the boy you are after hasn't grown his, he will very soon. If you touch his hair, you'll be poisoned by flesh-eating insects."

"I will strike quickly while the boy is vulnerable," the bug said, tapping his chin. He rubbed his back legs together and produced some excited clicks. The cicadas in the woods echoed with their own snapping song.

"Our children also have deadly venom in their

stingers," Doogan said, pouring on the nonsense as thick as he could.

"Hmm. They're like the offspring on Tantemar Prime. Wicked beasties they were, but no match for my people. We turned their hive planet to dust in less than a year."

Kraven took a pair of goggles from his bag and scanned the valley.

"Your planet smells delicious," Kraven said. "Nemeth is a foul place. Everything is sour. It has taken too long to conquer, as well. Many of my brothers and sisters wish to abandon it, but Command is too full of pride. They worry what the galaxy will think if the Plague is shooed away like common house pests, but this world . . ."

Kraven trailed off as he scanned the horizon. While he was distracted, Doogan snatched the fallen branch off the ground. It was thick and heavy, just what he needed, and he swung it right into Kraven's back. The monster doubled over, allowing Doogan to clobber him again on his gruesome head. Kraven fell to the ground, silent and unconscious.

Doogan dropped the club and ran. He had to get back to town and warn everyone, but he was no farther than a couple of steps when he heard Kraven's back legs clicking and the sound of enormous wings coming up fast from behind. When he turned, he saw

Kraven screeching in rage. Doogan yelped and tripped over Roger's huge feet. He tumbled down a hill and fell end over end, unable to stop himself. Eventually he got to the bottom and scrambled to his feet.

"You can't outrun me!" Kraven shouted.

I'm gonna try! Fueled by adrenaline, the principal ran faster than he had since he was nine years old.

Suddenly he heard a *THUNK!* and watched Kraven's body sail past him. The insect slammed into a tree and slumped to the ground. Surprised, Doogan turned and saw the robot, the one that kept invading his memories. Only, it was real and towering over him, swinging its arms around like it was in a boxing match.

"You!" Doogan cried.

"Hey, good to see you again. Listen. I ruined your pants and I feel awful about it," the robot said. "I want to make it up to you, but— Oh, hold on, here he comes."

Kraven got to his feet and charged at them. The robot picked Mr. Doogan off the ground and set him aside.

"Let me just put you right *zzzack* here while the bug and I have a little chat," the robot continued.

Highbeam pulled his fist back and planted it right beneath Sin Kraven's mandibles. The impact sent the bug off its feet and crashing onto its back.

"Unless you want another, I'd stay down," the robot said.

The bug wasn't hurt long. He unfastened a weapon from a holster and aimed it at the robot. It looked like a giant squirt gun, but the wave of blue energy that came out of it proved it was no toy. It hit the robot squarely in the chest, sending him crashing through three trees until he finally slammed into the ground.

"So we're playing rough, huh?" Highbeam said as he slowly stood. "All right—activate *demolition mode!*"

Doogan watched the robot's head sink between his shoulders. A yellow warning light flashed on his chest and his enormous arms spun like pinwheels. He stomped forward until *CLUNK!* His arms locked in place and the sound of a mighty engine whined to a halt.

"Aaargh!" the robot shouted. "Stupid glitch! Why is this happening to me?"

Kraven fired his weapon again. His aim was perfect and Highbeam was sent flailing backward, over the side of the cliff.

Kraven roared and turned the weapon on Mr. Doogan.

When the kids caught up to Highbeam, he was in the middle of an epic fight with Kraven. They watched in horror as the robot got his silver butt kicked. Kraven's weapon was just too powerful. Finn gasped as Highbeam went flying off the cliff edge. And then the monster turned his fury on Mr. Doogan.

"We have to do something," Kate said.

"Like what?" Lincoln said. "Stab him with your fluffy unicorn horn?"

"If you knew anything about unicorns, you would know they do what's right even when it's scary." Kate put up her hoodie so the golden horn bobbed back and forth. She looked ready to charge Kraven. Finn grabbed her arm and pulled her back down.

"When we get home, I'm telling Mom to stop letting you watch that show!"

"She's got the right idea, but there's a smarter way to do it. Finn, you and Lincoln circle around that way and try to get behind him," Julep said as she searched the ground, picking up rocks and examining each until she found a few she liked. "Kate, you come with me. When he's distracted, you boys tackle him."

"Tackle him?" Finn cried.

"Meh. I should throw the rocks. I have lots of experience," Lincoln argued.

Julep shook her head. "I had the best arm in North Carolina. I'm throwing the rocks."

The team split up. Kate and Julep scurried through the trees, doing their best to stay out of sight. Finn and Lincoln did the same in the opposite direction. All the while, they could hear Kraven shouting at Mr. Doogan.

"If you do not cooperate, you are of no use to me!" the bug roared. "I will kill you now, though it is a shame. Your plump body would harvest many strong hoppers."

"Don't worry, derp. I'll tackle him. You stay put," Lincoln whispered when they were directly behind Kraven.

"What? Why?"

"You don't want your girlfriend to see you get hurt," Lincoln said.

"I don't know what you're talking about," Finn said, but he knew his bright red face was giving him away.

"Every time you talk to her, you ramble. You're tripping over your own feet, and you keep staring at her. I'd laugh if it wasn't so pathetic. Do you think someone like Julep Li could like you? You're a coward and soft and—"

"I'm not a coward!" he said.

"Really? How come you never stand up to me?" Lincoln said. "I beat you up every day. You never fight back."

Before Finn could argue, he heard a *zing* in the air, followed by a *clink!* Julep was already tossing rocks. Kraven looked around, confused and irritated.

"Even your girlfriend is braver than you," Lincoln said.

Furious, Finn leaped to his feet and ran toward the locust, eager to prove Lincoln wrong.

"Finn! Wait!" Julep cried, but it was too late. Kraven heard him coming and pointed his weapon right in Finn's face.

"You!" Kraven hissed. "You're the boy who stole my weapon!"

"Finn Foley? That can't be right!" Mr. Doogan cried.

"He works with the Resistance! He is a thief and a spy!"

"You have to run, Finn!"

"I can't," Finn said, then pointed to the lunchbox in the creature's hand. "You have something that belongs to me."

Kraven made a noise that sounded like a laugh but came out wet and disgusting.

"Are you going to take it, Earth boy?" the bug said. He pressed a button on the side of his weapon and an engine hummed.

"I was hoping you might just hand it over," Finn said.

Kraven charged, knocking him to the ground. He pressed his weapon to Finn's forehead and hissed.

"Leave him alone!" Kate shouted as she stepped out of the woods. Julep followed. Lincoln did the same.

"If you move any closer, I will kill your friend!" Kraven shouted. "Where is the rest of the machine?"

Finn opened his jacket and lifted his shirt, revealing the blinking object.

"I'd give it to you, but I'm sort of attached," he said, then with a slap of his hand, he hit it squarely in the middle. The zap took his breath away, but it was worth it. He was no longer beneath Kraven. He was standing right behind him. With a swift kick, he planted his foot in what looked like the monster's butt. Pain rocked his leg as his toes connected with Kraven's hard exoskeleton.

The bug spun around and fired his weapon, missing Finn by inches. Panicked, Finn slapped the object again. This time he appeared next to Mr. Doogan.

"I'm very sorry about your office," he told the principal.

"We can talk about that later, Finn," he said. "That thing wants to kill you."

Kraven charged again. Finn slapped his chest and *zap!* He found himself behind the alien, close enough to snatch the lunchbox out of its grasp.

"I've got it!" he cheered, but his voice was drowned out by the rumbling of the lunchbox. It bounced around in his hand, forcing him to hold on tight. There was an ear-pounding flush, and the zipper slid open. Lightning flew out, and another whirlpool appeared.

"Not again, earthling!" Kraven shouted. He grabbed

hold of Finn's jacket and together they tumbled into the tunnel.

Finn's first trip into a wormhole was far from smooth, but this one was a roller-coaster. He and Kraven flipped end over end and spun like tops, unable to right themselves. Kraven didn't seem to enjoy it, either. He shrieked and tried to protect his eyes, letting go of his weapon. Finn watched it spin off in another direction, lost forever.

The landing was rough and knocked the wind out of him, but after a few moments Finn found his breath and got to his feet. The first thing he noticed was the tall red grass, then the sky above with its odd yellow hue. The air smelled like burning tires. The name *Terot* appeared in Finn's mind, the same way he knew Highbeam's home world was called Nemeth. Only, unlike Nemeth, Terot came with a sense of dread. A tickling fear crept up his throat. This was not a good place to be.

A drum boomed in the distance, pounding out a frightening rhythm. A horn and then a cheer and finally the growing sound of a stampede heading in his direction.

He closed his eyes to concentrate, hoping it would activate the lunchbox again, but Kraven's claw clenched tightly around his arm and distracted him. Finn couldn't jerk away.

"Where have you taken us?" the monster said.

"Let me go!" Finn demanded.

"You're not abandoning me here," Kraven roared.

Finn didn't know how he knew it, but what was coming toward them was worse than taking Kraven back to Earth.

Terot is a world where people and reptiles work together, hunting anything intelligent. They have a taste for brains, which they believe give them the power and intelligence of their victims.

Again, he closed his eyes and focused on home. He heard the familiar flush and felt a wind blast him as a new wormhole appeared.

As Kraven struggled to stand, a spear crashed near his tail. A wild-eyed creature dressed in furs and leather was riding on the back of what looked like a horse-sized dinosaur. Behind it were hundreds more.

Finn pushed the bug into the whirlpool. The tunnel entrance closed, snapping off the tip of a second spear. It didn't stop the weapon. The sharp point chased them across the universe. Finn realized that when they came out of the tunnel, the spear would, too. It might hit him or, worse, one of his friends. He had little time to act. Maneuvering himself in front of Sin Kraven, he used the bug as a shield, and when the duo shot out, the tip stabbed Kraven's leg. He screeched in agony as a fountain of foul-smelling blood spilled onto the forest floor.

Kraven stumbled forward, clawing blindly at everything. Somehow he managed to find Mr. Doogan, and with his wings extended, the two flew into the air, sloppily dipping up and down, clipping the tops of trees until they faded into the horizon.

Then Highbeam crawled up the side of the cliff. There was a smoldering hole in his Hawaiian shirt.

"What did I miss?"

12

The sky was thick with black clouds, as if it were angry with them for losing Kraven. A boom of thunder announced a torrent of rain. It fell on the group in sheets.

The kids and Highbeam ran down the trail and back toward the town. Lincoln's house was closest, and Julep led them there without asking for permission. It was fancy, maybe the nicest house in all of Cold Spring. White columns held up the front porch. There was an enormous picture window that looked out on the lawn. It was so neat and tidy it seemed as if every blade had been cut with toe clippers. There was an in-ground swimming pool in the backyard with a slide and a waterfall, a koi pond stocked with fat, orange fish, and a four-car garage. At the sidewalk, Lincoln stopped them all and told them to wait.

"C'mon!" Highbeam complained. "We're in a typhoon. My circuits are soaked!"

Lincoln ignored him. He walked over to the house and peeked through a window.

"He's so weird," Finn said.

"Something is going on with him," Julep said. "When I found him this morning, he was sleeping outside in a deck chair."

Lincoln gestured for everyone to follow him past the fence into a small bungalow painted with blue and white stripes. Once inside, Lincoln threw everyone a towel. They dried off among the pool toys with the smell of chlorine in their noses.

"Why can't we go inside your house?" Kate said.

"Because I don't like you," Lincoln said. "And Seth is home."

"Who's Seth?" Finn asked. Lincoln's eyes went to his feet. He didn't answer, and Finn decided not to press him.

"Nice pool. We used to have one back in North Carolina," Julep said.

"We did, too," Kate said. "I miss it."

Finn remembered the pool. His family spent long, lazy days floating in it. He and his dad used to have cannonball competitions to see who could make the biggest splash.

"All right, kid. This has been fun and all, but it's time to take me home," Highbeam said as he opened the compartment on his chest and took out the lunchbox. "Fire this thing up and let's go."

"Wait! You mean you're going to another planet?" Lincoln said, suddenly curious.

"We're really doing this?" Julep said.

Highbeam shook his head. "We? No, I—"

"I'm in!" Kate interrupted.

Finn looked at all the eager faces.

"Um, you might want to skip this. The trip is going to give you nightmares," Finn said. When he took the lunchbox, the little bungalow started to shake.

"No fair," Kate protested. "I'm going, too."

Highbeam tossed his towel on the floor. "There's a desert on Nemeth with a mountain—"

"Leah?" Finn asked, the name appearing in his head. Images of it pushed their way into his imagination. It was a dry, sunbaked landscape teeming with life. Billions of multicolored lizards lived there on its rocky cliffs, and tiny purple and white flowers defied the heat and sprouted in patches in every direction. Somehow Finn also knew the mountain had an "unusual ecological structure," though he didn't know what that meant or why it kept rolling through his thoughts.

"That's the place, little man," Highbeam said. "How did you know that?"

"Every time I think about using the lunchbox, I get bombarded with information. How can I know so much about places I've never been?"

"The gizmo was full of data about every known planet. When it fused to you, it must have downloaded all of it into your noggin. You're like a walking library of the universe."

"I'm so jealous," Julep said.

"Don't be. It's weird," Finn grumbled.

"Stop the bellyaching. I need you to focus on Leah. The mountain there is hollow. Can you have the gizmo drop us off inside it?"

"Wait," Julep said as she took her phone out of her pocket and polished the camera screen with her towel. Her face looked happy and nervous all at once. "I want to be ready for this."

Finn closed his eyes tight. He felt the lid of the lunchbox open, heard electricity crackle all around him, and felt a sudden blast of warm air. When he opened his eyes, a wormhole was waiting, growing bigger and bigger by the second. Without warning, it swallowed all five of them.

Finn's third trip through the cosmos wasn't much better than the first two, but at least he got to enjoy watching Lincoln scream in horror. The group flashed past planets and through the hearts of stars, around ocean-covered moons, and a giant world with a purple atmosphere. Kate covered her eyes until Finn took one of her hands.

"It's almost over!" he shouted to her.

"I hope not! This is amazing," Julep cried.

"I like her!" the robot shouted.

The wormhole dumped the group out onto the floor of a tall, circular room with shiny white walls. They went up dozens of stories, so high Finn couldn't see the ceiling. Cut into them were rows and rows of oval windows about six feet tall in height. As he clambered to his feet, he realized people occupied them, though the term *people* didn't seem like the right word. Some of them had more than one head. One looked like a pile of Jell-O with bones and organs visible through pink, jiggling flesh. Another seemed to have a body made from stacks of stones. There was a painfully thin gray person with an enormous head and eyes, and a soft pink creature held aloft by puffs of gas that came out of holes on its hands, legs, and bottom. There were some covered in fur and feathers and fins. No two creatures were the same.

While everyone gawked at the strangers, Lincoln leaned over and barfed.

"Ugh, space travel is hard on a belly," he groaned.

"Welcome to Nemeth," Highbeam said. "And the secret headquarters of the Resistance! Leah is a sanctuary for survivors of the Plague, and a center for planning our fight against them. Those people in the windows are the last survivors of planets that fell beneath the bugs."

"But there are hundreds of them," Finn said.

Highbeam's face formed a frown.

"Like I said. The gizmo could turn the tide for us, kid."

A door in the wall slid aside and three bizarre beings entered the room. The first was as hulking as a gorilla, only hairless and twice as big. He crouched on his knuckles as he lumbered along the floor. Next was a short, plump woman without legs. Her fluttering wings beat so quickly they were almost invisible and kept her afloat. She reminded Finn of a honeybee, the way she buzzed. Between them, wearing a long purple robe, was a tall and thin person with a long face. He had a slit for a nose, a huge, gaping mouth that never closed, and no eyes. A long, serpentine tail curled around his legs and moved as if it had a mind of its own.

"Invaders in the theater! Alert the guards," the go-rilla man barked as he pounded on his chest.

Highbeam stepped forward and tried to speak, but a blaring alarm drowned him out. Not long after, a small army of soldiers charged into the room with their weapons drawn. Like the observers, each guard was a different species; an alligator man, a woman covered in beautiful red feathers, and an enormous yellow cat. They demanded Finn and his friends put their hands in the air.

"Whoa!" Highbeam cried. "We're on the same team. I'm Highbeam Silverman, trained and *zzzeeeck* as-signed to the Plague mothership with my partner, Dax Dargon."

"Big guy?"

Standing in an open doorway was the same blue-skinned girl Finn saw during his first visit to Nemeth.

Highbeam's face glowed as bright as a sun. The girl rushed to him and he wrapped her up in a huge hug and swung her around, laughing and cheering.

"You're alive!" he cried.

"Awww, a few dopey bugs can't kill a daughter of Longdar City!" Dax said with a laugh. "So, you made it to Earth in one piece! I knew it!"

"Most of me did," Highbeam said. "I lost a J-23 in the wormhole. It's *zzzaaack* causing me some problems!"

"That girl has blue skin," Lincoln said.

"Mind blown," Julep whispered as she took a photo of the reunion.

"That dude has a fish for a head," Lincoln said.

"That lady's body is inside a glass of water!" Kate cried.

"Pardon the interruption." A voice boomed through the room, though it didn't seem to come from anyone. Finn was certain he heard it inside his head. "This celebration might be more appropriate if the rest of us knew what was going on!"

Dax approached the man in purple robes and bowed with respect.

"My apologies, Commander Teague," she said. "This is my partner, Highbeam—the one I told you about. He and I stole the wormhole weapon from the Plague. I sent him to Earth to hide it and he has returned."

The robot stepped forward and bowed as well.

"Sir, it's a great honor to—"

Teague held up a hand—a hand with a huge eyeball on the palm. It spun and focused on the group.

"That dude has eyeballs on his hands!" Lincoln said.

"Can you stop shouting out everything you see?" Finn whispered.

"And these children?" Commander Teague said.

"This is Finn Foley, from Earth," Highbeam said,

"and his sister, Kate, and friends Julep Li and Lincoln Sidana."

"We're not friends," the boys said in unison.

"Is it safe to assume these children have some connection to the wormhole technology?"

"Yes, sir," Highbeam said.

""I am Commander Miles Teague, last of the Ares, a once proud and noble people. Your efforts to aid our struggle are most appreciated."

"When it's really bright outside, how do you wear sunglasses?" Lincoln asked.

"I am going to strangle you!" Finn shouted at him. The room grew silent. Every eye landed on him and the tops of his ears burned with embarrassment. "Sorry."

"What a derp!" Lincoln said with a laugh.

"Where is the weapon, Agent Highbeam?" Commander Teague asked.

"Well, that's kind of a thing. You see, one half of it is stuck on Finn, and *zzzack* the other is fused inside of his lunchbox," Highbeam said. "The good news is it works when we put them together and the kid seems to be able to control it. The bad news is we can't get it off of him."

The bee girl zipped around Teague and buzzed in a language Finn didn't understand, though Teague followed every word.

"I couldn't agree more," Teague said as he turned to the gorilla-man. "Your thoughts, Ezekiel."

"Speaking to the Alcherian makes sense to me," Ezekiel said, then growled and hooted.

Teague raised his hands to those watching from above.

"We will suspend our scheduled discussions for today," he said.

The crowd murmured unhappily and stepped away from the windows.

"Follow me," Ezekiel said, and he lumbered out of the room. He led the group, including Dax, Teague, and the bee girl, through a sliding door and down a long hallway.

"Where are they taking us?" Kate asked.

"To see one of the big brains—an Alcherian," Dax explained. "Their world was famous for its technological geniuses."

"It was also famous for its arrogant know-it-alls," Highbeam muttered.

Teague stopped at a doorway with a red overhead light and extended his hands. The door magically slid open for them.

"Telekinesis!" Julep squealed.

Beyond was a laboratory with gadgets stacked to the ceiling. Glass containers full of bubbling chemicals were neglected on desks, and electronics littered tables and the floor. Small furry creatures in cages squeaked for attention, and on one entire wall was a massive digital screen crowded with equations, random notes, and arrows pointing in every direction. The rest of the room was littered with half-empty cups and dirty dishes, and at the center of it all was an extremely obese and pale creature, sweating like a garden hose was tucked under its clothes. It had more eyes than Finn could count and was eating a bowl of what looked like noodles. As they got closer Finn realized they were purple worms, all of which were very much alive.

"Pre'at, your attention is required," Commander Teague said.

"I am on my lunch break," the scientist said in a high-pitched voice.

"This is urgent!" Ezekiel grunted.

Pre'at slammed her spoon on the table, spilling some of the worms onto her workspace. She got to her feet and turned all her angry eyes on the group.

"If you people were always this pushy, Alcheria might still exist!"

She squinted, then pressed a button on her belt. Lenses came out of her clothes and swung over each eye. "What is this? More refugees? Don't think you're going to house them in my lab. I won't stand for it!"

"She looks like an ice cream cone with googly eyes glued to it," Lincoln said.

"Everything that comes into your head does not have to come out of our mouth," Finn said to him.

"They are not refugees, Pre'at. They may very well be the answer to our prayers. This is Agent Highbeam, who has returned from the planet Earth with a valuable weapon that might change the course of our struggle," Teague explained.

"Well, get to the point. My brain is exceedingly powerful, but I don't read minds without my mental helmet," she said as she scanned her lab. "Which I have momentarily misplaced."

Highbeam nudged Finn forward. "Show her."

Finn lifted his shirt so the scientist could see the device.

"It creates wormholes," Commander Teague explained.

"Nonsense! Wormholes are fantasy."

"Not according to Einstein and Rosen," Julep said. She reached into her backpack and took out a book on astrophysics, shaking it at the strange alien scientist.

"It works. I've used it myself," Highbeam said.

"It made me barf," Lincoln said.

The bee girl buzzed.

"Of course I can see it's fused to him," Pre'at said as she peered closer at Finn. She snatched something off her desk that looked like a remote for a television and waved it over his chest. The lights inside the machine came alive. "Intriguing! You are correct. I suppose I would have invented this myself if I wasn't so busy with my other work."

"Can you get it off of me?" Finn asked her.

"Of course I can," Pre'at said. "You'll die. Is that a problem?"

"Wait, what?" Finn cried.

"The machine is not stuck on you—it's stuck *in* you. It has fused into your DNA. It's fascinating. And you can control the device with your thoughts?"

Finn nodded.

"Well, this opens up so many practical applications. Imagine if we could rebuild this machine and fuse it to soldiers."

"Pre'at, can you focus on the kid?" Dax asked.

"Yes, I can remove it and keep him alive. Not immediately, but I can do it. I need time to study it, though. The boy must remain here in my lab."

"For how long?" Highbeam asked.

"It's hard to say. I could figure it out in a day, or it could take years," the scientist said.

"Years? I can't stay here for years," Finn said.

"He's got school and homework," Kate said.

"Children, these are desperate times," Commander Teague said, turning to Highbeam. "Food, ammunition, and transports are all in short supply. If we don't find a way to turn the tide of this war, we will be crushed.

A machine that makes wormholes is exactly what we need. Make the children listen to reason."

"We're eleven years old. We don't have to listen to anything," Lincoln said.

"If he won't stay willingly, then we will have him arrested," Ezekiel said.

Highbeam stepped between the aliens and Finn.

"Now, everyone simmer down. The kid came here to help us."

"Yeah! We were told you were the good guys," Julep said.

"We are!" Highbeam said.

"Dude, we can't trust these people. Let's go home," Lincoln whispered to Finn.

Julep nodded in agreement. So did Kate.

Frustrated, Finn couldn't argue. Things were going wrong, and he had to do something before he was the guinea pig of a giant bowl of vanilla pudding. He guessed it would be worse than spending the rest of his life hiding an alien technology under his shirt. He closed his eyes to focus on home, but Teague spoke again.

"We are the good guys. Pre'at, take scans of both parts of the machine. I trust your advanced intellect will find good use for them. When you are finished, Finn and his friends will return to Earth."

Pre'at grumbled but scanned Finn's chest, then the lunchbox.

"Thank you, Commander," Highbeam said. "Julep, do you want to tell everyone about the rift?"

She stepped forward and explained to everyone her theory about the open wormhole tunnel, and along with Highbeam shared the bad news that Sin Kraven had found his way to Earth.

"It would be pretty great if you could find a way to close it," Kate said.

"That might be a problem," Dax said. "When Finn showed up, he distracted Kraven and his soldiers. I took the opportunity to make a run for it, and on the way I fired one last sonic blast. It hit a fusion dumpster and *boom!* The whole neighborhood is poisoned. It got his soldiers, but I guess the Major survived, probably from falling into the rift."

"Agent Dargon, select some soldiers and guard that alley so no one else finds this rift," Commander Teague ordered. "Agent Highbeam, you will return to Earth with the children."

"You want me to go back?" Highbeam cried.

"Someone has to capture Kraven and bring him back here," Teague explained. "You have the most experience on Earth. Meanwhile, Pre'at will find a solution to the boy's predicament."

Highbeam's face ignited with digital flames, but he said nothing.

"I'll tell Goldplate and the kids what's going on," Dax promised. "I'll keep them safe until you get back."

"Thank you."

Finn turned to Highbeam. "I'm sorry."

"It's not your fault, little man," the robot said. "Let's go and get this done so I can get back."

Finn held the lunchbox in front of him. He felt the floor shake, and a second later the group was dragged into a new tunnel. Before they knew it they were back in Lincoln's bungalow.

Highbeam snatched a pool net off the wall and snapped it over his knee.

"This is so *zzzzack* messed up." The robot stormed out into the rain.

Finn chased after him. "Where are you going?"

"Just leave me alone right now, kid. I have to go break something!" Highbeam said. He sprinted ahead and vanished into the woods.

When Finn returned to the bungalow, Lincoln was arguing with the girls.

"Listen, Highbeam is dumb for trusting those weirdos," he said. "You could see they were keeping something from him."

"They're his friends," Julep argued.

"No they're not," Lincoln said.

"What do you know about friends?" Finn said. "You don't have any."

Lincoln's face turned as red as a tomato.

"You know what? Wormholes suck. Aliens suck. You guys suck, and so does my life since I met you," he railed. "Go home and leave me alone!"

"Boy, he got angry all of a sudden," Kate said when she, Finn, and Julep went outside.

"Yeah, he does that," Finn said.

"Listen, I'm going home," Kate said. "Lucia is coming over, and I need some time to calm down about what I just saw before she gets there."

Finn made her promise to be careful before she raced off.

"Walk me home, Finn Foley," Julep said.

He felt his mouth dry up and sweat roll down his neck. He tried to tell himself that it was caused by all the crazy things he'd just experienced, but he knew better. Julep was the reason.

"So how many eyeballs did that lady have?" she asked.

He shrugged. He couldn't seem to talk.

"Did you see the man with the shark fin on his head?"

He nodded.

"I wonder how that guy with the fish face breathes."

He shrugged.

"Are you going to be all right?"

"I—I—" He didn't know what to say, and she didn't push him.

"Finn Foley, this was the best day ever! Thank you! We were the first kids to explore outer space. We saw dozens of alien races. We witnessed telekinesis. We talked to a lady that was part honeybee!" she said.

"You didn't think it was too weird?"

Julep smiled. "Weird is where you want to be."

They stopped in front of a house. It wasn't fancy like Lincoln's. It actually reminded him of his except for a long steel ramp that went from the front door to the driveway. Coming down it were Julep's parents and a teenage boy supporting himself on metal canes. Each step was a struggle, but he managed to get to a van parked in the driveway. Julep's dad slid the passenger-side door open and helped his son into a seat.

Julep said goodbye and rushed off to join her family. He watched as she leaned over and gave the teenage boy a kiss on the cheek. Finn guessed he was Julep's older brother. The teenager laughed and whispered something into her ear, which made her turn pink.

"Shut up!" she cried.

As Finn headed home, he tried to see his life through Julep's eyes. Maybe having a machine that could take him anywhere in the universe wasn't such a bad thing. It let him spend the day with Julep Li!

"Are you Finn Foley?" a voice asked.

Finn glanced over and saw a sheriff's car roll up next to the curb. Inside were two deputies. Lincoln was in the back seat, shaking his head at him in disgust.

"Yes."

"We'd like you to come with us. We have a few questions we want to ask you about your missing principal."

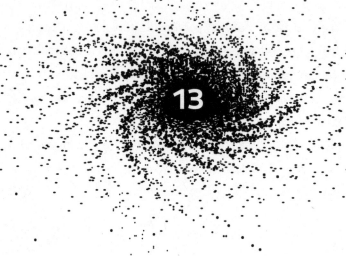

13

The interrogation room at the sheriff's station didn't look like the ones in movies, with a table and metal chair and the lightbulb hanging in the criminal's eyes. This one had a sofa and a window. It was nice and comfortable.

The deputies introduced themselves. Deputy Day had a warm, friendly face, covered in freckles. Deputy Dortch's square jaw and piercing eyes were intimidating. He studied them, the way an owl might watch a mouse.

"We've called your parents," Deputy Dortch said. "They're on their way."

"Why?" Finn asked.

"It's department policy to have a parent present whenever we question kids," Day explained.

"Makes it easier for them to say goodbye to you if we lock you up," Deputy Dortch said.

The boys looked at one another and grimaced.

"We don't have to do the good cop/bad cop thing with them," Day said. "They're kids."

"They could be kids who have committed a crime," Dortch argued.

The door opened and a thin woman dressed like a fashion model barged into the room. She shot Lincoln an angry look, then turned to the deputies.

"What did he do this time?"

"Now, let's not jump to conclusions," a man said as he followed. He looked a lot like Lincoln, only taller, leaner, and fit. His hair was perfectly combed and he wore a suit and tie.

"You must be Mr. and Mrs. Sidana," Deputy Day said.

"Not yet," the woman said, showing off a diamond engagement ring. "I'm Nadia, Dr. Sidana's fiancée."

"I'm Lincoln's dad."

"He's an MD," Nadia bragged. "A surgeon."

There was another knock and Finn's mom and Kate entered. They both looked bewildered.

"I'm Sloane Foley, Finn's mother. What happened? Finn, are you hurt?" Mom said, rushing to his side.

"I'm fine," Finn said, slightly embarrassed.

"Hello, Mrs. Foley. I'm Deputy Day. I'm sorry to

alarm you. I know it must feel scary to get a call from the sheriff's department, but—"

"Oh, we've been expecting this call for a very long time," Nadia said as she turned to face Lincoln. "So, it's finally come to this? Your father is too soft on you. Goodness knows I haven't been able to help steer you in the right direction. I guess it's up to the police now."

Lincoln's dad took a deep breath but didn't say anything in his son's defense. Sympathy crept into Finn's heart, but he quickly pushed it out. Lincoln Sidana was the king of the jerks. He didn't deserve sympathy.

"Actually, Lincoln and Finn aren't in trouble," Deputy Day said.

"We're not?" Finn said.

"At least, not that we know about," Dortch said as he eyed the boys suspiciously.

"Last night we were called to the elementary school to investigate vandalism in Principal Brian Doogan's office, but since then we've come to believe he may be in bigger trouble," Day explained. "He's disappeared. His car is in the staff parking lot, and he didn't return home last night."

"We suspect he's been kidnapped," Deputy Dortch said.

"Kidnapped?" Mom cried.

"Who would kidnap an elementary school principal?" Dr. Sidana asked.

"That's what we're trying to find out," Deputy Day said.

"This is terrible news, but what does it have to do with our kids?" Finn's mom asked.

"We were told the boys spent most of the day in his office," Dortch said.

"What? Why?" Lincoln's dad asked.

"Fighting," Lincoln said matter-of-factly.

His father shook his head in frustration. Behind him, Nadia wore a smug smile.

Finn's mom was not so calm. Her eyes flashed hot with anger.

"Finbar Foley! You lied straight to my face."

"Finbar." Lincoln laughed until he snorted.

"I didn't lie," Finn cried.

"Not telling me is the same as a lie! I thought we were past all this! You can't get kicked out of another school."

"What?" Lincoln cried. "You've been expelled before?"

"Mom, it's all his fault," Kate said as she pointed at Lincoln. "He's been picking on Finn, and he didn't tell you because he's been trying to stay out of trouble."

"Is that true?" Lincoln's father demanded.

Lincoln shrugged.

"I don't get it. Lincoln was at our house last night,"

Mom said, then turned to Lincoln. "Were you pretending to be nice and polite? Did you come over just to give my son a black eye?"

"No," Lincoln said, and for a moment he seemed to be ashamed of himself.

"Wait! *You* gave him that black eye?" Lincoln's father said.

"He gave me mine!" Lincoln cried.

"You left the house without asking, too!" his father yelled. "You know better than that!"

"He must have done it when we were at the fundraiser, Bikram. Poor Seth!" Nadia said, turning to the deputies. "Seth is my son from my first marriage. He's such a good kid, a star athlete, a great student. I had hoped he would be a role model to Lincoln. I bet he was worried sick! You're lucky to have a brother like him."

"He's not my brother," Lincoln seethed. "And you're not my mom!"

"Seth and I try and try with you, but you don't want to be part of this family. You would rather hang out with another troublemaker."

"Whoa!" Finn's mom spun around on Nadia. "My son is not a troublemaker!"

Nadia squeaked in fright and took a step back.

"Finn went through a tough time when his dad and I split up, but he's been trying to get back on track. I don't know what this fighting is all about, but he is a good kid."

"Folks, let's calm down," Deputy Day said. "Like I said, Finn and Lincoln aren't here because of trouble at the school. We need to focus on Mr. Doogan. The boys may be the last people to have seen him."

"Which makes them suspects," Deputy Dortch said.

Deputy Day sighed.

"Boys, did you see anything unusual at school yesterday? Perhaps a stranger on campus?"

Finn and Lincoln shared a look. Yes, they saw a stranger on campus—a seven-foot-tall one made of metal that steals people's clothes—but they shook their heads. Finn felt terrible about lying to the deputies, but what was he supposed to say? *A giant locust from outer space kidnapped the principal. Oh, and he's got a laser gun, so consider him armed and dangerous.* It was better to let Highbeam find the big bug, and when he did, Mr. Doogan could come home.

The deputies asked a few more questions—what Mr. Doogan's mood was when they saw him last, what time it was, and what he was wearing. Then they thanked them.

"I have to apologize for my partner," Deputy Day said when she walked everyone outside. "This is his first week on the job, and he's really eager to do his best. I think he's seen a few too many cop movies, but he means well."

She gave everyone a business card in case they remembered anything, and then went back inside. When she was gone, Lincoln's father turned to Finn's mother.

"Lincoln is a good kid, too," his father said. "It's only lately that he's been acting out. In some strange way, I'm kind of glad he snuck out last night. I haven't been able to get him out of his room in months. He's been a loner for a long time, and though I don't like that they're fighting, friendships can start in strange ways. I own a boat with a guy from med school that I used to hate. Now our families plan vacations together."

Mom laughed. "My oldest friends were the meanest girls I ever met."

"Maybe Mr. Doogan's a genius for locking them in his office."

"Well, if they can promise to stop giving each other black eyes, Lincoln is welcome at my home anytime," she said.

"Let's not go that far," Finn muttered.

"I know this is last-minute, but I'm thinking we should follow the principal's example and get these kids together more often. Come over for dinner tonight. We'd love to have you," Lincoln's dad said.

"Bikram?" Nadia said with a whimper.

"We would love to," his mom said, turning to give Finn a look that said "This is your punishment."

Dr. Sidana gave her the address just as two more deputies entered the station.

"Did you just hear that last dispatch call?" one of them said.

"About the giant grasshopper?"

"Yeah, apparently it stole an ice cream truck with the help of a teddy bear," the deputy said with a laugh.

"I guess Halloween is coming early to Cold Spring," the second deputy said.

Finn, Lincoln, and Kate shared a knowing look.

Kraven was in town.

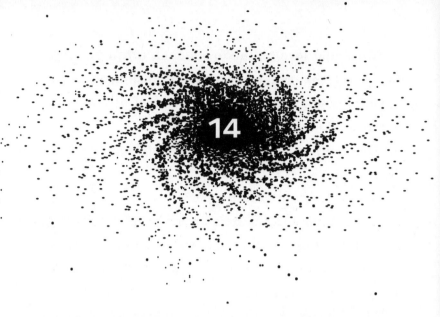

14

Principal Doogan drove the stolen ice cream truck through town while Kraven gorged himself on frozen treats and complained bitterly about his injuries. He was torn on what to do. If he drove to a busy part of town, someone might get hurt. Kraven was unpredictable; violently angry at times. Doogan couldn't be sure the bug wouldn't kill someone if they got in his way. He decided it was best to stay as far from innocent bystanders as possible.

Kraven finished his feast, then forced his body into the front seat. He was covered in sprinkles and caramel sauce. He peered into his goggles as they drove down Route 9.

"This machine will make finding the boy easier," Kraven said.

"You don't get it," Doogan burst out. "You're a giant bug riding around in an ice cream truck. Someone is going to notice you eventually."

The locust patted the weapon on his hip. Mr. Doogan saw what it did to the robot and shuddered. What if he fired it at a person?

A few cars passed without incident. A couple of teenagers pulled up alongside, gawked at them, and then cheered. One took pictures with his phone.

"Those Halloween costumes are sick!" the teenagers shouted just before their car sped away.

"The Plague will make quick work of conquering this planet," Kraven said. "You have no defense system, and as far as I can tell, earthlings are all morons. How would this world fight off an interstellar invasion?"

"We have fleets of fire-breathing dragons," the principal said, continuing his lies.

"Just like on the silver moon of Perleen. Their beasts did not prevent their defeat," the bug bragged.

"Well, dragons are just the first line of defense," Mr. Doogan said. "We have wizards, a whole school of them, plus a summer camp for the children of gods. Not to mention mutant superheroes and the Jedi."

"Stop!"

Doogan slammed on the brakes. The truck was now stopped outside a video game store. Posters advertised the latest games, and a steady stream of kids was coming in and out.

"What is this place?" the bug demanded.

"It's a store that sells . . . it's where our hoppers come to buy training programs that make them better killers."

"The boy I seek may be inside," Kraven said.

Before Doogan could stop him, the bug was out of the truck and marching into the store.

"No!" he shouted, chasing after him. He was sure he would be met by the screams of terrified kids, but once inside he found a crowd circling the monster and taking selfies.

"So cool!"

"I can't believe you're here!" a kid said, pointing to a display for a game called *John Hopper 4: Garden of Death*. There was a massive poster for the game on the wall, as well as a giant cardboard cutout of a heavily armed grasshopper leaping into battle.

"Did you know we were having a John Hopper instore appearance today?" one clerk asked another.

"Nope. Dude, that costume is so realistic."

"You are not him," Kraven said as he picked up each kid and studied his or her face. "You are too small. You seem to be female. I am hunting the male of your species. Where is the boy who calls himself Finn?"

Kraven waved his hand over a lens sewn into his

jacket. A projection turned the store into a 3-D movie. The crowd *oohed* and *ahhed* as an alien city appeared. There in a dusty alleyway a woman with blue skin lay on the ground with her back against a dumpster. Next to her was a pile of robot parts that seemed vaguely familiar to Mr. Doogan. The girl tossed them into a strange, swirling hole in the air, while Kraven and a group of bugs just like him fired their weapons at her. When all the parts were gone, there was a flash of light and a boy stepped out of the hole. It was Finn Foley.

"Finn, what have you gotten yourself into?" he whispered.

"This Earth boy is wanted dead or alive by the Plague Armada," Kraven said. "Do any of you know him or the location of his fortress? He is hiding, no doubt, most likely lying in wait to attack me with his venomous stinger."

The kids cheered.

"This is awesome!" the clerk cried.

"Dad, you have to buy me this!" a kid cried, rushing through the store with the game in her hand. There was a mad rush for the display, and the rest of the crowd tore it apart trying to get the last few copies.

"This is the greatest day of my life!" a little boy cried. He reached over and gave Kraven a hug. "You're my hero!"

A girl rushed over to Mr. Doogan.

"What game are you from?" she asked.

15

"**P**ut on something nice, brush your teeth, and comb your hair," Mom shouted up the stairs. It was time to leave for their dinner at Lincoln's house. Finn and Kate were moving like sloths. Neither one of them wanted to go.

"We're really doing this?" Finn asked. He stood at the top of the steps, waiting for his mom to say it was just a joke intended to teach him a lesson. "If I have the option of being grounded, I will happily take it."

"Yes, we're doing this. Tell your sister she is not allowed to go full unicorn tonight."

"Seriously?" Kate shouted from inside her room. "Hold on. I have to change!"

When everyone was ready, Mom looked them over

and nodded her approval. They piled into the car and picked up a cherry pie from the bakery.

"Why are we bringing dessert? Didn't they invite us?" Kate asked.

"It is nice to bring something when you are invited to dinner and making new friends," Mom explained.

"New friends? This is a one-time-only thing," Finn cried.

"Who knows?" Mom said. "If you and Lincoln can't learn to get along, we might be eating with the Sidanas all the time."

Finn groaned.

"Have you heard from Highbeam?" Kate whispered to him in the backseat.

Finn shook his head. He stared out the window as the sun set on the town and wondered where the robot had gone. The clouds promised more rain. He hoped Highbeam would be all right.

"Both of you are calling a truce in the Finn-versus-Kate war. I don't want to give Nadia any reasons to turn her nose up at us," Mom said when she parked outside of Lincoln's house. Everyone got out of the car, and Mom smoothed imaginary wrinkles from her skirt, then adjusted Finn's collar.

She rang the doorbell. A tall, handsome teenager answered. He looked just like Nadia, with coal-black eyes and perfect hair. He smiled, showing off a set of sparkling white teeth.

"Mom! They're here," he said. "I'm Seth. Come on in."

Nadia materialized, wearing a sparkly silver dress like she was on her way to a New Year's Eve party. She eyed the family up and down and forced a smile.

"And they brought a pie," Nadia said, though it came out sounding like *they brought a sack of dog poo.* "We're so happy you could make it."

Dr. Sidana appeared and took everyone's jackets. "This is going to be fun," he promised after he called for Lincoln.

The inside of the house was as beautiful as the outside. The hardwood floors gleamed. The art on the walls looked valuable. The furniture was so nice Finn was hesitant to sit down.

"I hope you like vegetable masala," Bikram said. "It's a family recipe and one of Lincoln's favorites. It's also vegetarian night around here. We do it once a week."

"As long as it doesn't have pineapple and ham, I'll love it," Kate said.

The grown-ups talked about the weather, the president, and the legendary pothole on South Street. Finn and Kate took a seat on the sofa. Seth slid in between them, wearing a huge smile.

"So, I hear you're the one who gave Chunky his black eye," he said.

"Chunky?" Finn asked.

Lincoln came into the room wearing a shirt and tie. He tugged on his collar like it was strangling him. He looked miserable.

"Is it true? Did this little guy give you that shiner?" Seth asked him.

"Let's eat," Bikram said. He flashed Seth a "cut it out" look, but the teenager either didn't notice or decided to ignore it.

The families gathered at a massive table. Nadia explained the dull history of where they'd found it (Portugal) and the even duller story of how they'd had it shipped to Cold Spring. When she wasn't rattling on about the fancy furniture, she talked about the upcoming wedding and the honeymoon.

"We're spending most of it in Mexico—Cancún, Tulum . . . ," she said.

Mom smiled. "Sounds lovely."

"I let him plan it," Nadia said. "I don't really care where we go as long as there's shopping. We'll be gone for two and a half weeks."

"Are the boys going with you?" Mom asked.

Nadia laughed. "Oh, no! We're leaving them here. Bikram's brother will check in on them, but I think Seth is old enough to look after them both."

Lincoln slammed his hand on the table and jumped to his feet.

"You never told me this!"

His father tried to calm him.

"Lincoln—"

"I'm not hungry anymore," he said.

"That's a first," Seth whispered loud enough for Finn to hear. Finn noticed Nadia laugh at her son's mean joke.

"Lincoln, please," his dad begged, but Lincoln marched out of the room and through a sliding door that led to the pool.

"He's so cranky, and honestly, who can ever guess what it's about?" Nadia held up a dish. "More masala?"

Finn felt Kate kick him under the table. "Go see what's wrong," she mouthed at him.

Finn could see Lincoln standing near the pool, sulking. Did his sister really think he wanted to help him feel better? Seth was worse than Lincoln, but he was also proof that there was justice in the world. The biggest bully at his school had a bully all his own.

She kicked him again, this time much harder. He shot daggers at her and rubbed his shin. He knew if he didn't go he'd have bruises up and down both legs by the end of the night.

"I'll be right back," he told everyone, and a moment later he was outside standing next to Lincoln. Together they looked down into the pool.

"So . . ."

"What do you want, derp?"

"Nothing! I just . . . are you okay?"

"What do you care? Leave me alone!"

"I don't know why I bothered!" Finn seethed and turned to storm back into the house, only to find Seth standing behind him.

"Why are you out here?" he asked, talking in a baby voice. "Is Chunky upset? Is he going to cry?"

"Leave me alone, Seth," Lincoln muttered.

Seth put Lincoln in a headlock and squeezed.

"How did you like sleeping outside last night?" Seth said. "I bet the mosquitoes ate well. That's what you get for sneaking out on me."

"Let go!" Lincoln demanded. He struggled to break the older boy's grip, but Seth was bigger and stronger. He wrenched Lincoln's neck hard, causing him to cry out in pain.

"You're trying to get me in trouble with your dad. That's not cool, Chunky. If you do something like that again, I'll feed you another underwear sandwich. I know how much you like them. I bet your mom used to make them for you."

"Don't talk about my mom!" Lincoln roared. He fought as hard as he could but Seth would not let him go.

Finn had never seen anyone abuse Lincoln. He wouldn't have thought it was possible that morning.

His neck and ears were rubbed raw from the struggle. His lower lip was split. Blood smeared his chin.

"Let him go," Finn said.

Seth's eyes locked onto him.

"Keep your stupid nose out of it."

"You heard what I said. Let him go." He tried to sound tough, but his voice was shaking. Seth was nearly twice his size.

Seth pushed Lincoln and he fell to the concrete. He turned his attention to Finn and snatched him by the collar.

"Does that school you go to teach you to be stupid?" he said.

Stupid. Seth spit the word out of his mouth like it was something disgusting. Finn suddenly understood why it made Lincoln so angry. In fact, he thought he understood more about him than ever before. The underwear in his lunch, the things that made him mad, his reluctance to let anyone into his house when it was raining. Lincoln was a jerk because of Seth.

"You heard the kid," a voice said behind them.

Seth spun around to face the stranger, only to get an electrical zap that caused him to collapse like a marionette. Standing behind him was Highbeam.

"Never cared much for bullies," the robot said to Lincoln. "Are you okay, kid?"

"Why are you two here?" Lincoln raged. "Go away!

Get out of my life!" Lincoln bellowed. He was near tears.

"We were trying to help," Finn cried.

"I don't need your help," Lincoln said.

"Have it your way," Highbeam said, then turned to Finn. "I'll meet you at your house. I've got a plan to capture Kraven, but I need a change of clothes."

When the robot disappeared into the dark, Lincoln dragged Seth's unconscious body onto a deck chair and slapped him a few times across the face. When Seth didn't wake up, Lincoln slipped a pair of sunglasses on him and tried to prop him up into a sitting position. It didn't help. Seth's head bobbed up and down, and a long trail of drool escaped the corner of his mouth.

Finn left Lincoln there. He had tried, a lot more than Lincoln ever would if the situation was reversed. He walked back into the house and found the parents were wrapping up dinner.

Everyone said their goodbyes, and Finn and Kate followed Mom out to the car. Rain fell in a drizzle and the air was cool. They were shivering and complained loudly for her to turn up the heat. Instead, she turned in her seat to face them.

"I need the two of you to hear me. There can't be any more secrets. I know you lie to me because you think you're protecting me, but I'm the grown-up and I fix the problems. All this tiptoeing around the house like

I'm going to break stops today. I am not going to fall apart, and neither is this family as long as we stick together. I know this year was the worst, but we survived it, and we'll survive the next year and the next. We are doing just fine. I know it's not perfect, but I'd take this family over that one any day of the week. Those people are miserable."

"We're not really going to their house for dinner every week, are we?" Finn asked.

"Are you kidding? I couldn't spend another minute with that woman," Mom said. "Or her phony teenage son!"

Finn smiled. It was nice to know she could see through people other than him.

Finn and Kate found Highbeam lying on Finn's bed reading another comic book. He was wearing a Modest Mouse concert T-shirt and a pair of sweatshorts that barely stretched over his wide hips. It was obvious he found them in the boxes in Mom's closet.

"Have you read this? Now he can freeze things with his breath," the robot said as he shook the comic. "Pffft!" He threw it in disgust.

"Feeling better?" Finn asked him.

"I'm sorry I ran off. When I get *zzzeeeck* angry, the only thing I can do to feel like myself is demolish something. There's a whole patch of forest up on the mountain that will never be the same."

"I know you didn't want to come back here," Finn said.

"I've got kids and *zzzack* I was expecting to see them," Highbeam said. "But Teague is right. The war is going badly. People are losing faith. We need that weapon if we hope to have any chance against the bugs."

"Are you sure you can trust him?" Kate asked.

Finn was surprised to hear her echo Lincoln's opinion.

"Teague? Sure! He built the Resistance from nothing. I trust him with my life."

"Well, you might be in trouble for sticking up for me. If you hadn't done it, you might be with your kids right now."

Highbeam placed his big metal hand on Finn's shoulder. Finn was surprised by how good it felt and how disappointed he was when the robot took it away. "When my kids hear this story, they'll understand. Their father lives by a code, and turning his back on a friend isn't part of it."

"So tomorrow we find Kraven," Finn said.

Highbeam nodded.

"In the meantime, I have some questions about unicorns," Kate said.

"Oh, I don't know, little lady," Highbeam said. "It's not appropriate as a bedtime story."

"You tell me what you know right now!" Kate cried as she crawled into Finn's bed. "I'm seven. This is very important to me!"

"All right, simmer down. Now, unicorns used to be all over the universe, frolicking and farting rainbows."

"Farting rainbows?"

"He's teasing," Finn said.

"No, I'm not. *Zzaaack!* They literally pass rainbows out of their behinds."

Kate's eyes widened.

"Five hundred years ago the Xenithian Blood Empire went from planet to planet and captured them."

"No!" Kate said.

"Yes! The Empire trained them for use in their wars. Now most of the cosmos trembles when they hear them coming."

"That's not true! Unicorns are sweet and kind," Kate whimpered.

"A unicorn is a horse with a dagger on its head. Those things run around impaling people. And the worst part is *zzzack* how they laugh about it later. Well, long story short, they rose up and massacred the Xenithians."

"Massacred?" Kate whimpered.

"Yeah, it's a real gory story, but they're free now. I mean, the training has changed them forever. They still fart rainbows, but it's not as cute as before, especially if they're stabbing someone in the face."

Kate was silent for a long time. Finn couldn't read her expression. It seemed to roll through cycles of surprise, despair, confusion, embarrassment, and something that looked like she really needed to use the bathroom.

"I need to be alone," she said, and walked out of the room.

"Dude, I think you broke my sister," Finn said. "Do you know what unicorns mean to little girls on this planet?"

"I warned her the story would ruin it for her. Listen, I need to power down and recharge my batteries." A compartment on his chest opened, and from inside he removed a small phone-sized object and the pink lunchbox. He placed both on Finn's bedside table. "Take these. I will probably head out before you wake up, but this will let us communicate if there's an emergency. Just say my name into this end, and it will connect you to me. The readout will even tell you where I am."

"Wait! I'm not going with you? I want to help."

"That's a big no-no. You need to hunker down here and stay out of sight. He knows what you look like, little man. Besides, if I go up on the mountain and find him, I need you to get a wormhole ready to toss him through."

"Kraven isn't on the mountain. He's in a stolen ice cream truck with Mr. Doogan. They're somewhere in the town. It's better for me to go look for them. If people see you, they will freak out."

"There's a man dressed as a rodent and a giant locust cruising around in a truck made of ice cream," Highbeam said. "I doubt anyone will notice me."

The robot's face dimmed as he powered down.

"The truck isn't made of ice cream," Finn tried to explain, but Highbeam's face was already empty.

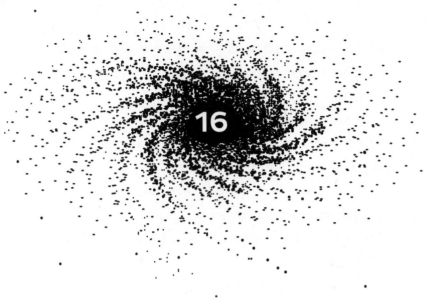

16

In the morning, Highbeam was gone, and Mom was knocking on Finn's bedroom door.

"I'm going into the office this morning for a little bit," she said. "You have to watch your sister, and before you give me any lip about it—"

"It's cool, Mom," he interrupted. "I like having her around."

She eyed him oddly, then smiled. As she hurried down the stairs, Kate appeared. A garbage bag was slung over her shoulder.

"What's that?" he asked.

"Unicorn stuff."

"You're throwing it out?"

"I'm not feeling it anymore," she said.

"I'm sorry. Highbeam should have kept his mouth shut about them," he said.

She gave him a defeated shrug.

"Just tell him that if he knows anything horrible about kittens he should keep it to himself. By the way, did you see who's in the backyard?"

Finn looked out his window. Lincoln was there, lying on his back on the lawn.

A moment later Finn was standing over him.

"Why are you here, Lincoln?"

"My dad took Nadia into the city." Lincoln pulled a couple of blades of grass out at the roots and tore them into smaller pieces.

"Leaving you alone with Seth. Is he picking on you again?"

"In between trips to the toilet," Lincoln said. "Remind me to thank Buckethead for shocking him. Listen, I know I was kind of a jerk—"

"Kind of?"

"Okay. I suck. Can I just hang out here?" Lincoln looked small and pathetic. Another flame of sympathy sparked inside Finn's heart, this one too big to stamp out.

"You hungry?"

Lincoln nodded.

"Come on."

Lincoln got to his feet and followed him into the

house. Finn tossed two frozen waffles into the toaster and handed Lincoln a banana. He had one himself and poured them both a glass of milk. When the waffles were done, Lincoln used so much syrup they were swimming. He swiped a butter knife out of the drawer and sliced his banana to make a smiley face on top. When he caught Finn's eye he shrugged.

"Don't judge," he said. "My mom used to make them like this."

"Where is she?"

"She died when I was five."

Finn put two more waffles in the toaster for himself and used the time to try to figure out what to say. Nothing sounded right, so he decided to keep quiet. There weren't words for such a thing.

"Where's your dad?" Lincoln asked.

"I honestly don't know."

"That sucks," Lincoln said. It sounded sincere.

Finn nodded. "Yeah, it all sucks. One day he just walked out, and we haven't seen him since."

"And that's why you got kicked out of your last school?"

Finn nodded. It was hard to talk about without feeling a little ashamed. He made some dumb decisions back then because he was always angry.

"Where's Buckethead?"

"Looking for Kraven," Finn explained.

Lincoln went back to his breakfast. He took a couple of bites, then set his fork down and looked at Finn.

"What do you do for fun around here?"

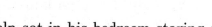

Finn and Lincoln sat in his bedroom staring at each other.

"This is fun," Lincoln said.

"You came to me," Finn said.

"Don't you have any video games?"

"Yeah," he said.

"Can we play them?"

"Nope. How long do you plan to stay?"

"Hey! What's this?" Lincoln asked, picking up the weapon Sin Kraven left behind when he came through the lunchbox.

"Put it down! It's dangerous," Finn said, grabbing it away.

"What does it do?" Lincoln grabbed it back.

"I don't know."

"Then how do you know it's dangerous?"

"Maybe 'cause it belongs to an evil alien from outer space?" Finn shouted.

Lincoln gazed at the weapon, then at Finn, then at the weapon again, and then at Finn one more time. A mischievous smile stretched across his face.

"Just hear me out."

"No," Finn said.

"The monster bug is in our town, right? Shouldn't we capture him?"

"I'm not listening to you."

"Buckethead can't do it by himself. You saw what happened when he tried. Plus, Mr. Doogan needs our help!" Lincoln looked down at the weapon, smiling. "Foley, this is your fault and you're going to let the principal suffer?"

"My fault? It's *our* fault!"

"Okay, I'll take fifty percent of the blame. I'd like to use fifty percent of this big honking laser gun to make it right."

The boys wrestled for control of the weapon, but Lincoln was stronger. Once he had it in his hands, he raced out of the room and was outside before Finn could stop him.

Finn hurled himself down the stairs and was reaching for the door when Kate stepped in his way.

"I'm bored. Want to play UNO?" she asked.

"Kate, stay here. I'll be right back," he said, trying to get around her.

"Uh-uh! Mom said you can't go anywhere without me."

Finn watched Lincoln climb onto his bike in the front yard.

"Get your jacket," he said. "And the lunchbox."

"This is a very bad idea," Finn cried as he and Kate pedaled their bikes to catch up with Lincoln.

"No, derp. This is an excellent idea," Lincoln yelled over his shoulder. "Maybe the best idea in the history of ideas. Besides, what kind of kid are you, anyway? I can't believe you've had this sitting inside your house and haven't tried it."

"We're going to get in trouble!"

"You *need* some trouble, Foley! If we help catch the alien, you can take him back to Crazy World, where everyone is made out of butterscotch and fish parts! Dr. Creepy Yogurt Lady will take that off of you. Isn't that what you want?"

"He's got a point," Kate said.

"No, he doesn't! He just wants to shoot that thing," Finn cried.

"Where's the ON button?" Lincoln shouted.

"See?"

As they steered toward downtown, a familiar jingle drifted into their ears. It was a song they had heard all their lives, a happy and catchy tune that announced the coming of the ice cream truck.

They stared at one another in disbelief.

"Do you think—?" Kate began.

Lincoln nodded.

"C'mon!" Finn said, and the trio tore off in the direction of the music. While they pedaled, he reached into his pocket for Highbeam's transmitter and held it to his mouth.

"I want to talk to Highbeam."

"What's that?" Kate asked.

"Some kind of space walkie-talkie," Finn explained. "Highbeam gave it to me."

"Where's mine?" Lincoln cried.

The transmitter vibrated, and the readout said *Recipient: Highbeam Silverman. Location: The top of Bear Mountain.*

"Kid, is that you? What's that music I hear?"

"We're chasing Kraven through the town right now!"

"I told you to stay home!"

"I know. It's a long story. We're getting close to the village," Finn said. "Near the big church."

"Sorry, I'm visiting from outer space. I have no idea where that is," Highbeam cried.

"Just follow the music!"

17

"The hoppers did not attack with their stingers," Kraven said as Doogan steered the truck through the town.

"They only come out when they sense a threat," the principal said. "It's best to stay calm when you're around our children. No sudden movements, no waving your big laser gun around—just nice and calm."

"Good advice, earthling," the bug said. "When the Plague conquer this world, I may choose to keep you alive. Some of my colleagues train and fight our captives in a battle pit. I believe you would do well."

Kraven dug through the coolers for more treats. "If only the rest of your kind were as wise," he continued. "None of those hoppers could tell me where to find the boy. Perhaps they are hiding him. We must go back and torture the truth out of them!"

The bug yanked the wheel, causing the truck to scrape a parked car. Doogan frantically steered it away.

"NO!" he cried. "I will steer the truck. The cars are actually robots in disguise! If we hit one it will transform and attack us."

Kraven peered at the passing cars. "This is a very strange world," he muttered.

Doogan knew if they kept driving through town, something terrible would happen. There was only one choice left. He made a turn at Fishkill Road and pointed the ice cream truck toward Bear Mountain. The roads up there were steep, overlooking high cliffs.

He would drive the truck off of one. It was the only way to stop Kraven and keep Finn Foley safe.

He made another right, then slammed on the brakes. There were three kids on bikes blocking the road.

The sudden stop caused Kraven to fly forward. His head smacked hard against the windshield. When he shook off the pain and confusion, he let out an angry roar.

"It's him!" he shouted, pointing at the kids.

Mr. Doogan peered at the trio. Kraven was right. Finn Foley was one of them, along with Lincoln Sidana.

The bug tried to force his bulky body out of the truck, but his wings got caught in the doorway.

"Run!" Mr. Doogan shouted, but the kids didn't budge. Instead, Lincoln got off his bike and lifted a strange machine onto his shoulders.

He aimed it right at the truck.

When Lincoln eased the weapon onto his shoulder, a harness slid out of the bottom. It adjusted itself to fit him perfectly.

"Fancy," Lincoln said.

"What do you think you're doing?" Finn said.

"Swatting a bug."

"If you blow up the town, I'm going to be mad," Kate said as she got off her bike. "I live here."

"She's right, Lincoln," Finn said. "You're fooling around with something you don't understand."

"I know. I'm eleven. That's what we do."

There was a whirling sound that grew louder and louder as Lincoln's smile grew bigger and bigger. A wave of energy came out of the weapon, followed by a sonic boom, and an invisible force slammed into the ice cream truck. The vehicle flew backward, sliding down the road fifty yards before it stopped, leaving a trail of burned tire tracks.

The kickback sent Lincoln tumbling end over end into a mailbox. Finn and Kate pedaled to his side. They were both sure he was dead.

"That was SICK!" Lincoln shouted when he opened his eyes. "I call dibs on the space bazooka. You got the robot."

"I didn't get the robot. You dumped him on me," Finn said.

"Um, the truck is coming!" Kate said, pointing down the road. The ice cream truck was barreling in their direction. This time Kraven was behind the wheel.

"Make room, Finbar." Lincoln propped himself on the back of Finn's bike, facing in the opposite direction. He put the weapon on his shoulder.

"Kate, go home!" Finn cried.

"No! Mom said we have to stay together!"

Finn pumped the pedals hard, with Kate doing the same. The roads were slippery from the previous night's rain, and Finn struggled to keep the bike balanced with Lincoln's extra weight.

"Dude, you're all over the road! I'm trying to aim back here," Lincoln shouted.

"Don't fire while I'm—"

BOOM! The force of the blast caused the bike to leave the ground. It came down hard, but Finn managed to keep it upright.

"I missed!" Lincoln said. "Uh-oh, here he comes."

Finn looked over his shoulder. The ice cream truck was nearly on top of them.

Inside the truck Mr. Doogan balled up his fist and punched Kraven in the face. There was a cracking sound, and he felt fire swim up his arm. He was pretty sure he'd broken his hand.

"You are a foolish creature," Kraven hissed as he struggled to steer.

"I won't let you hurt those kids."

"Oh, are you the appointed guardian of the young?" the bug asked.

"Yes! I'm a principal!"

"You serve no purpose to me," the bug said, and with a vicious swipe, Kraven's sharp claws ripped open the belly of the Roger the Fighting Raccoon costume. Cotton stuffing poured out onto the floor.

Kraven scooped up some of the fluffy filling and studied it intensely.

"Explain this!"

"It's a costume—a symbol of my school—the fighting raccoon," Doogan said, hoping he sounded braver than he felt.

"A ceremonial armor, I see. You wear it when you go to battle. This school you speak of is a battle station of some kind?"

"Yes, a school is a battle station," Doogan told him. "We have an army of millions in mine. Invaders are shown no mercy. We attack with books and pro-tractors. We put our victims in detention and some-times Saturday school and assign them hours and hours of brutal homework. Do you think one over-grown insect is any match for the fighting raccoons? We drink the blood of the fallen so they can join our undead army!"

Doogan grabbed the wheel, and this time he steered into a parked car, missing the kids by inches. They crashed and were violently bounced around inside. The truck was totaled.

Kraven dragged himself out onto the street with Doogan right behind him. The principal jumped on the bug's back and wrestled him to the ground. They fought on the wet pavement, though it wasn't long before the bug had the upper hand. He flipped the principal onto his back and, with a deadly claw, looked prepared to slice the man in two.

And then, without warning, a huge silver foot punted the bug off of him. Mr. Doogan looked up at his hero. The robot was back. It smiled its strange digital smile at him.

"Hey, partner. It's so weird how we keep running into each other."

The robot stomped toward Kraven with its fists raised. He slugged the bug in the mandibles, and he fell to the ground. The punch was followed with a knee to the face and then a kick in the gut. The bug sprang to his feet, delivering his own brutal punches, knocking the robot backward several feet with each blow. Cars slowed as they watched them exchange one vicious shot after another.

"Are you people making a movie or something?" a woman asked as she passed.

The robot snatched the locust off the ground by the neck and held him there. It looked to Doogan as if he had won the fight. Kraven was helpless, unable to break free as he flailed wildly, but it didn't last. He whipped his tail across the robot's chest, knocking him off balance. Kraven was free.

"Demo-mode!" Highbeam shouted, and his head sank between his shoulders. A yellow light flashed on his chest, and his arms started to spin like windmills. There was a loud *CLUNK!* and the robot froze in place, his arms and legs locked.

Kraven used Highbeam's moment of weakness to drill the robot with punches. He shoved his claws into his enemy's gut and pulled out wiring. He tore an arm off, then hit him so hard the robot's head flew off its shoulders. The rest of his body fell into a pile in the street.

"No!" Finn cried.

Desperate, he snatched the weapon out of Lincoln's

hands, hefted it onto his shoulders, and pointed it at the locust.

"Step back!" he shouted.

Kraven turned his horrible eyes on Finn.

"If you fire that at me, you will kill the principal," the monster said as he pulled Doogan to his feet to use him as a shield.

Frustrated, Finn lowered the weapon.

Kraven wrapped an arm around Doogan's chest and extended his wings, and once again Finn was forced to watch the two of them fly away.

Kraven and Mr. Doogan soared over the tree line, higher and higher, but the principal was no longer afraid of falling. It was time to stop the bug once and for all. He slammed his elbow into Kraven's neck.

"Fool! You can't stop me!" Kraven shouted. "Your ridiculous efforts to be a hero mean nothing. I have killed thousands of heroes. In days I won't remember your face any more than I can remember the others!"

Kraven reached into his jacket and took out something that looked like a grenade. He pulled a pin and a clock started ticking down from ten. Doogan knew it was now or never. With all his strength, he wrestled with the bug until he was on his back. The wind blasted his face, making it almost impossible to see, but he didn't need his eyes. With his good hand he punched the tender space between Kraven's wings. The monster shrieked and dropped his weapon.

BOOM! It ignited the forest below.

Doogan didn't stop his attack. He punched the soft spot again and again and heard Kraven's pained cries get louder and louder. "If you're smart you'll leave this planet! And when you get back home, tell your ugly people not to mess with a fighting raccoon!"

Without warning they dropped out of the sky and into the Hudson River. The water was shockingly cold and it filled the mascot costume, weighing it down and pulling Doogan toward the river bottom. He clawed at the zipper as the light above grew dimmer, but his big paws were not cooperating. Worse, the lack of air made his chest tighten, and he saw stars. With his lungs nearly empty, he gave the zipper one final tug. *POP!* The front of the costume opened wide. He struggled out, and with everything left in him he swam to the surface, gasping for air.

As he recovered, Mr. Doogan watched Kraven rocket out of the river. He was helpless to stop him as the monster steered toward the town. Doogan's body could take no more. He was cold, wet, beaten, and exhausted, and with the waves lapping in his ears, he passed out.

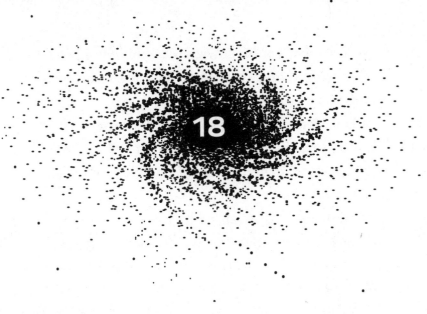

18

The kids knelt in the street by the pile of metal limbs that was once their friend. Kate sobbed. Lincoln picked up the robot's head and frowned. "Awww, Buckethead." Finn stood in stunned silence. He knew Kraven was dangerous, but Highbeam seemed larger than life, even indestructible.

There was a screech of tires and everyone looked up to see a van come to a stop. The door slid aside and Julep jumped out, grabbed one of Highbeam's legs, and tossed it inside.

"Load him into the van. The police will be here any minute!" she cried.

The kids did as they were told. Some of the parts were super heavy, but they managed, and still had room for the bikes and the big alien weapon. Only when they were pulling away did Finn notice Julep's brother was driving. He thought back to the day before, seeing him on his crutches.

Julep seemed to read his mind. "Our van is tricked out so Truman can drive it," she explained.

"Can we trust him to keep this quiet?" Finn whispered.

"Truman's cool," Julep said.

"She keeps me up to date on all her weird investigations. Except this is the first time one of them has been real," Truman said over his shoulder.

"They're all real," Julep said. "I have just never found any evidence."

"How did you know we needed help?" Lincoln asked Julep.

"I get an alert on my phone whenever anyone posts anything on the internet with certain key words— *robot, alien, Sasquatch, chupacabra,* you know. Someone posted a pic of Kraven at the video game store. Truman offered to drive me over so I could take a look. Big and ugly was definitely there, but he was long gone. We were on our way back home when I got another alert."

She showed Lincoln her phone. The screen said "robot fighting giant locust."

Truman drove them to Finn's house. Luckily, Finn's

mom was still at work, so he wouldn't have to explain the robot parts. Finn opened the garage door and spread a tarp on the floor, then he and the others gingerly set Highbeam on it one piece at a time.

"Okay, guys, good luck," Truman said before driving off.

Lincoln closed the garage door and everyone gathered around the tarp.

"What are we going to do?" Lincoln asked.

"I'm thinking," Finn said.

"You should take him home, back to Nemeth. You said he has a family. They would want him back," Kate said.

She tried to hand Finn the lunchbox, but he waved it away.

"I will, but I want to try to fix him first."

"Here you go again. Listen, derp, there are some things in life you just can't fix. He's a robot from an alien world, not a leaky faucet," Lincoln said. "You don't have a clue how he works."

"I fix stuff here all the time. When I don't know how to do something, I watch do-it-yourself videos."

"Do you think there are do-it-yourself videos for fixing him?" Lincoln asked.

Finn scooped Highbeam's head into his hands. He flipped it over, studying it.

Using Julep's phone, he went online and searched video after video, hoping to find something that might help. Machines were machines. Most of them worked the same way. He just had to find one that looked familiar.

Hours passed. Kate went inside. Most of the videos were of no help, but every once in a while Finn stumbled on something that was actually useful. Slowly but surely, he snapped body parts back into place while Lincoln and Julep watched. The most helpful videos had instructions on electrical wiring, and Finn was able to reconnect some of them. Still, there were tons more that hung loosely out of Highbeam's belly.

"What's up with your brother?" Lincoln asked Julep once the robot's legs were reattached. Highbeam was looking more like himself, though his head would not stay on his neck.

"He's sick," Julep said. "He has a rare disease that attacks the nerve endings that go from his brain to his limbs. The messages between them get jumbled. That's why he uses the canes. Sometimes he can't walk."

"Is there a cure?" Finn asked.

Julep shook her head.

"I'm sorry," he said.

"Truman is going to be fine," she said as if it were a fact. "There are doctors and scientists working on it every day. A cure is right around the corner. Don't feel sorry for him. Everybody's got a glitch."

"A glitch?" Lincoln echoed.

"An obstacle. You know, something you have to get around."

"My mom died when I was five. It was just me and my dad for a long time. Then he met Nadia," Lincoln said. "She and Seth moved in and everything changed. We used to have pictures of my mom all over the house, but Nadia wanted to take them down."

"Does your dad know how Seth treats you?"

"Nadia makes him happy," Lincoln said. "He was sad for so long."

"But now you're sad," Julep said.

"I guess that's my glitch."

"What about you, Finn?" Julep asked.

"I'm cool."

"I spilled my guts, and you're going to take a pass? Tell her about your dad."

"He walked out a year ago and I haven't heard from him since. He doesn't call. He doesn't write. He missed my birthday and all the holidays. He doesn't send money. He's just gone, and I can't even ask him why he left."

"Except you can," Julep said.

"What do you mean?"

"The lunchbox," Lincoln said. "You could use it to find him."

"I don't know where he is," Finn said.

"Use that walkie-talkie thing Highbeam gave you, dude."

Finn reached into his pocket and took out the transmitter.

"He said I could use it to find anyone, and it would even tell me where they are," Finn told Julep.

"What are you waiting for?" Julep asked.

Finn looked at them. "What would I say to him?"

"Ask him why he left," Julep said.

"Tell him he's a jerk!" Lincoln cried. "Yell at him. Tell him you're awesome and you don't need him. Tell him he's the worst dad in the world. I don't know. Dude, if I had a way to talk to my mom again, I wouldn't worry about what I was going to say. I'd just call."

"He's right," Julep said. "Just call."

Finn held the device to his mouth. Could it really work? Would it really let him talk to his dad? There was only one way to find out.

"I want to talk to Asher Foley," he whispered.

The device vibrated a couple of times, but nothing happened.

"Weird," Finn said.

"Try again," Julep said.

"Asher Foley," he repeated. The transmitter vibrated again, and this time Finn heard static on the other end. He also felt something happening underneath his shirt. The circuitry was lighting up like a fireworks display. Was it lending power to the transmitter to help send the message?

"Hello?" A voice broke through the static. It was gruff and distant and sounded slightly confused, but it was unmistakably his father.

"Dad?"

"Finn?" The voice cracked and popped. "What's up, buddy? I haven't even gotten into the car."

There was a loud *WHOOSH!* And his dad's voice dropped in and out.

"Dad? Dad?" Finn shouted into the transmitter, but his father's voice did not return. "I've lost him."

"What did he mean about not even being in the car?" Julep asked.

"I have no idea," Finn said.

"Look at the screen," Lincoln said.

The transmitter flashed numbers: *8, 16.*

"What does that mean?" Julep asked.

Finn shrugged.

"C'mon," Julep said. She grabbed Finn by the arm and pulled him to his feet, then Lincoln.

"Where are we going?" Finn asked.

"To see your dad," Julep said. She snatched the lunchbox out of the compartment in Highbeam's torso and shoved it into Finn's hands.

"Oh, no! I'm not barfing on my shoes again," Lincoln said.

"C'mon, Lincoln. He needs us," Julep said. She took both boys by the hand and led them into the backyard.

Finn wasn't so sure he wanted to take the trip, either, but Julep looked so eager and confident. He held the lunchbox out in front of him and closed his eyes tight. "Take me to my dad!" he shouted, but nothing happened.

"Maybe you need to be more specific," Julep said.

"Take me to eight sixteen," Finn said, and he focused hard on the numbers flashing on the transmitter. They were pushed aside by his father's face, the way he looked the last day Finn saw him, with his dusty brown hair, easy smile, and big green eyes. He opened the front door to go to work, looked back, and gave Finn a smile.

"I'll see you later, buddy."

He was expecting a wormhole, but something very different appeared. When the flushing noise came, it was less like a toilet and more like a honk. There weren't any strands of electricity either, though Finn could feel an energy all around him. His hair stood on end, and without any warning a giant, golden bubble encased him and his friends.

"Derp? What's going on?" Lincoln asked.

"I have no idea," Finn said. "This has never happened before."

A hole appeared beneath them and they fell into it. There was a flash of blue light that blinded them, and a second later, they materialized in his backyard. Only, it wasn't his backyard in Cold Spring. It was the backyard of the house where he used to live, in Garrison, when his dad was still around.

"Well, at least I don't feel sick," Lincoln said.

"This is so strange," Julep said. She reached out and touched the skin of the golden bubble. It stretched against her finger like they were inside a balloon.

Finn did the same and felt a strange film pressing against his hand. It was spongy—and when he pushed, it pushed back. *POP!* A blast of wind whooshed over them, and suddenly they were free of the bubble.

"This is so weird," Julep asked.

"I agree. I—" Finn said, but he was interrupted by the sudden appearance of an old man. He limped across the lawn with numerous weapons strapped to his legs and arms, but the weirdest thing about him was the cowboy pajamas he wore over his clothes. They were made for a little kid and covered in happy cowboys riding ponies and jumping over tumbleweeds.

"Oh, boy. They're not going to like this," the old man said. "You're going to screw everything up. Go back home."

"I'm looking for my dad," Finn explained.

"Your dad is fine. Worry about yourself. The Rangers will be here any second. If they catch us, everything is ruined!" the old man cried.

"What are you talking about?" Julep asked. "And who are you?"

"Another time, kids," the old man said. "Now go. Oh, Finn. Listen to your sister! Her idea will save the world."

Before they could demand an explanation, another hole appeared beneath the golden sphere, and just like before they tumbled into it, only to be blinded by the brilliant blue light again. A moment later, the bubble popped. When Finn looked up, he found they were back at his home in Cold Spring, exactly where they started.

"Hey, derp. You're on fire," Lincoln said.

Finn heard something sizzling. It was . . . him. The machine on his chest was red-hot and burning through his clothes.

"Ahhhh!" he yelled, then jumped to his feet. He raced to the garden hose and turned on the faucet, soaking himself to cool the machine down. Steam rose off his body and into the air.

"Maybe that wasn't such a great idea after all," Julep said, turning off the water.

19

Finn didn't want to talk about what happened. It was too weird and too emotional. Dad, the weird old man, the fire—it made his stomach flip and flop. He decided to keep it from Kate. She would only want him to try again, and something told Finn he was messing with things he shouldn't. To take his mind off of it, he went back to work on Highbeam. Lincoln and Julep stayed for a while to try to help, but they seemed a little freaked out, as well. For the rest of the evening they were silent. When they were gone, Finn continued piecing together the parts of the robot until Kate brought him a sandwich.

"Any luck?" she asked.

"I've done everything I can," he said. "Which isn't much. His head won't stay on straight. The left arm is so beat up I don't think it will ever work again. And no matter how many wires I reconnect, there are a million more. I can't get any power to his systems. I'm worried he's gone."

"I'm sorry." Kate pulled the tarp up to Highbeam's chin. "He wouldn't want to be naked."

Mom was waiting for them in the living room when they finally decided to quit for the night.

"Finn, are you okay? You look like you lost your best friend," she said.

"It's been a long day."

She kissed the top of his head. "Get some rest. You have school tomorrow," she said.

He and Kate headed for the stairs.

"What? No arguments?" Mom asked them.

"I'm too tried to argue," Kate said.

"I never thought I'd see the day," Mom teased.

"I'm also too tired to stick my tongue out at you," Kate replied.

"Oh, hey! Did you hear they're making a movie in Cold Spring?" she called after them. "It's got robots and giant bugs in it. That's pretty exciting, huh? I think we should go down and watch them shoot it this week. Maybe we'll get discovered and have to move to Hollywood!"

Kate set the lunchbox on his nightstand, then padded off to bed. He sort of wished she'd sleep in his room. He gave his teeth a lazy brushing and then stood by his bedroom window and looked out into the night. Kraven was out there somewhere. Now that Highbeam was gone, Finn was going to have to destroy the monster all by himself. He just didn't know how.

Julep and Lincoln were back on his front steps bright and early the next morning. "You kids better get going," his mom said, shooing Finn out the door. "You're going to be late."

Finn threw his arms around her and hugged her tight.

"What's this all about?" she asked, laughing.

He pulled Kate in for another hug.

"Is this seriously happening right now?" Kate said, her voice muffled in his jacket.

"I just love you both very much," he said before running out the door.

The trio were half a block away before Lincoln spoke. "I love you, Mommy," he teased.

Finn shrugged. "I wanted them to know. I might never see them again."

"Now, why wouldn't you see them again, Finn Foley?" Julep asked.

"I have to confront Kraven," he admitted.

"So we're skipping school?" Lincoln's eyes lit up. "Aww, derp. I'm so proud of you."

"You two aren't coming with me," Finn said. "I have to do this on my own."

"You saw what that bug did to Highbeam," Julep said. "How do you plan to stop it when a seven-foot robot didn't stand a chance?"

"I've got the lunchbox, and if I get in trouble, I can always give this thing a smack and it will send me somewhere safe," Finn said, gently tapping his chest. "Plus, I brought these."

He opened his backpack to reveal several cans of bug spray.

"Dude, you can't be serious," Lincoln said, shaking his head.

"I am. If Kraven wants me, he's going to get a face full of poison. I just can't let anyone else get hurt," he said, hoping he sounded braver than he felt.

"At least let us help you prepare." Julep had two books in her backpack about bugs. She gave one to Lincoln, and they read aloud as they walked.

"What we need is to find a locust's natural predator," Julep said.

"Are there any planets that have giant killer wasps or lions as big as a truck?" Lincoln asked.

"I don't think so," Finn said.

"Hey, here's something," Julep said. "It's about Kraven's exoskeleton."

"That's tough stuff," Lincoln said. "Highbeam couldn't even crack it."

"It's not the exoskeleton we want to hurt. It's what's underneath. The rest of Kraven is just—well, he's like a s'more."

"A s'more?" Finn cringed.

"You know how when you toast marshmallow over a fire, the outside gets crunchy? Then you put it between the graham cracker and the chocolate and take a bite? The outside is hard, but it's gooey on the inside. That's Kraven's body."

"You just ruined s'mores for me forever," Finn moaned.

"Sorry," Julep said. "The point is that if you can get to the gooey part, you can hurt him—maybe even kill him."

"But how? His exoskeleton covers his whole body," Finn said.

"Not all of it. It's like one of those suits of armor the knights wore during the dark ages. It's made up of separate pieces and the pieces overlap. There are spaces between them, exposed parts. All you have to do is find one."

When they got to school, Finn took a deep breath. "Well, thanks for the help. I guess I'm going to try the trails up on the mountain again. Wish me luck."

"Well, do we get hugs, too?" Julep asked.

Finn's heart raced, but he gave Julep a hug, even if it was awkward and a little sweaty. When he turned to Lincoln he was surprised to find his former enemy with his arms outstretched. Finn shrugged and gave the boy a hug, too.

"Now!" Julep said.

Suddenly, the hug turned into a headlock.

"What are you doing?" Finn raged.

"You're not going anywhere, Foley," Lincoln said.

"We're sorry," Julep said. "But we can't let you go after Kraven alone."

Soon, a group of kids gathered around them to watch the struggle.

"Fight! Fight! Fight" they chanted while Finn tried to free himself.

"This isn't cool!" Finn shouted.

But Lincoln wouldn't let go. "If I have to beat you up to save your life, that's what I'm going to do, derp!"

Moments later, Finn, Lincoln, and Julep were sitting in Acting Principal Applebaum's office. She slammed her fist on the desk.

"THIS NONSENSE HAS TO STOP!"

She winced, as if her own voice had frightened her.

"I'm sorry for that outburst," she continued, then

turned her attention to Julep. "I've come to expect this sort of behavior from the boys, but Julep Li? I am shocked."

Julep's face turned pink with embarrassment.

"I simply do not have time for schoolyard fights. Mr. Doogan is missing, and I am in charge of everything. And right now I'm supposed to be at a retirement breakfast for Mrs. Green."

"Ms. Applebaum, you are absolutely right. We have been very immature. I think you should force us to sit in this room all day and think about our behavior," Lincoln said.

"Yes, I think that's an excellent idea." She got up from her desk and made her way to the door. "And you're not going anywhere until you're all friends."

"I can't believe I didn't see this coming," Finn grumbled when she was gone.

"You can be mad at us, Finn Foley," Julep said. "But we're in this together."

At that moment Deputy Day and Deputy Dortch were driving along the Hudson River. After two days of searching, Principal Doogan was still missing and the deputies didn't have a clue where he could be.

"It doesn't make sense as a kidnapping. There was no ransom note," Deputy Day said.

"Agreed," Deputy Dortch said, frowning. "We need to put some pressure on those boys. Put me in a room with them, and I'll have them spilling their guts within an hour."

"Avery, they're just kids," Deputy Day said.

"Kids are just criminals in smaller bodies."

"Dortch! Stop!"

"I'm serious, partner. Don't be fooled by their innocent smiles. I've looked into the face of evil before, and those kids looked just like it."

"No, I mean *stop*!"

Dortch slammed on the brakes, and the car came to a stop mere inches from Principal Doogan. He was standing in the road, shivering in his underwear and covered in bug bites.

"Mr. Doogan? Where have you been?" Deputy Day cried as she leaped out of the car.

"A giant bug from outer space kidnapped me against my will," Doogan said, gasping. "It's trying to kill one of my students. His name is Finn Foley and I have to save him. I know how this must sound, but you have to believe me."

"Let's get you in the car," Day said, taking him by the arm. "I think we should take you to the hospital. You can tell us about the alien invasion on the way."

"It's not an alien invasion," he said as Dortch helped

him into the back seat. "It's just one alien, shaped like a big grasshopper."

"Of course, of course," Day said.

"This is Car Four," Dortch said into the radio. "We've found Brian Doogan on Route Nine, east of town. We're taking him to the hospital. He needs medical attention."

"You've got to believe me!" Mr. Doogan said.

"We do," Deputy Dortch said, then gave his partner a knowing look.

The wind whipped at Kraven's wings, making it hard to fly straight, and with his still-blurry eyesight, he stopped frequently to readjust his path. Below, he could make out the fortresses of the Earth people, exposed where an invading force could easily destroy them. It was so arrogant, almost taunting. When he got home with the wormhole generator in hand, he would urge Command to make Earth its next conquest—even if it was only to teach these people a lesson.

But for now, he had to stay focused on finding the boy. If not for being impaled by a spear and then a headfirst collision in the ice cream truck, Kraven would have already killed him. Well, Finn's good fortune could not last forever. He was nearby. Kraven could almost smell him. Soon the weapon would be his.

He sorted through everything the principal told him about Earth. He mentioned children went to something called a school. It would have to be a big fortress to house all of them and an army of the undead, not to mention the dragons and the transforming robots. He flew over the town, looking for structures with weapons on the roofs, but he saw nothing. Would they really be so cocky as to not defend their hoppers?

He needed to get closer. He skimmed the ground, landing in the center of a road. Cars screeched to a stop around him. People screamed. He marched to the sidewalk and grabbed an old woman by the coat.

"Where is the battle dome you call a school?" he hissed.

The old woman fainted. He let her fall to the ground, then turned, looking for someone else, but everyone fled in terror. He wondered if he should head back to the river and find the principal. Pain might convince the man to reveal the location of the school, but before he could take flight, something slammed against his body. He was hurtled hard to the pavement. A huge yellow vehicle screeched to a stop. A door opened in the side and a man stepped out.

"I'm so sorry. I didn't see you. Are you—what are you?"

Kraven hissed as he got on his feet.

180

Understandably frightened, the driver got back inside the vehicle, closed the door, and sped away. Kraven was tempted to chase it down, but there was something on the back of the vehicle that stopped him in his tracks. It was a painting of a creature with a big furry body, a huge smile, and a mask over its eyes. From the neck down it looked very familiar.

What had the principal called himself? A fighting raccoon?

Kraven sprinted after the bus. His wings extended and lifted him into the air. He flapped with all his strength, until he was directly over it, then dropped and clung to the top.

"I am coming, boy," he said.

"Wake me up when this is over," Lincoln mumbled, then put his head down on Ms. Applebaum's desk.

"Tell me one reason why you two don't think I have a chance against Kraven!"

"You have the strength of a kitten," Lincoln said.

"Sometimes your brain isn't on speaking terms with your body," Julep said.

"You're slow."

"You have the reflexes of a scarecrow."

"When you get scared your nose whistles so loud Kraven would hear it a mile away."

"I said one," Finn grumbled. "Julep, give me the lunchbox."

Julep shook her head. She had her arms wrapped around it, and she wasn't letting go.

"Fine! I don't need it to get out of here." He gave his chest a smack. The zap came, and he vanished, but he didn't get far. He popped up in Ms. Applebaum's seat with his chest so hot he thought he might pass out.

"What's wrong?" Lincoln said.

"It's not acting right," Finn admitted.

"Good! You're stuck with us," Julep said.

Finn slapped it again. This time he appeared back in his original seat, and the machine was even hotter.

"Give me the lunchbox," Finn pleaded. "I need to make sure it works."

"How stupid do you think we are, derp?" Lincoln said.

Without warning, a figure dropped out of the sky and hovered in Ms. Applebaum's window. It was Sin Kraven.

"You!" the bug shouted.

"Give me the lunchbox!" Finn cried.

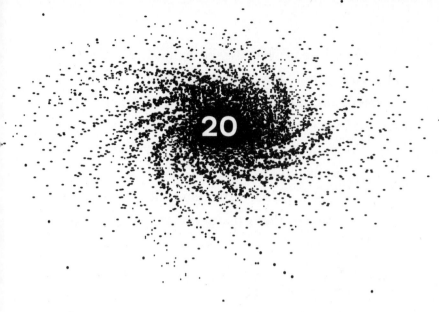

20

Mom got halfway to work before she realized she forgot her phone. She turned around and went home, parked the car and got out, right before she locked her keys inside it.

"This is going to be one of those days," she growled. There was an extra set in the kitchen, but her house keys were locked in the car. Luckily, she hid an extra set of those in an old coffee can in the garage.

She was in a hurry and meant to grab the keys and run, but the science fair project in the middle of the floor was so curious. She didn't realize her son was interested in science at all, and whatever he was building looked really elaborate. She'd just take a peek.

The tarp came off and she backed away, stunned and confused. It looked like some kind of robot.

"What in the world?" she said. The robot's head popped off and bounced across the floor. When it stopped, she heard a hum come from inside it, and watched as a stream of computer code raced across its glass face. The icons swirled into two perfect circles that suddenly blinked at her.

"Uh-oh," a voice said from inside it. *"Zzaaack!"*

Finn's mom screamed and ran out of the garage.

"That's not good. All right, body, I know you're a mess, but let's pull it together," Highbeam said. There was a zap of electricity and suddenly he was whole again. He stomped over to retrieve his head and put it where it belonged.

He swung his arms around, and then his legs. Nothing felt right. He walked back and forth to test himself out, but his right leg dragged behind him.

"Activate Repair Mode," he said, and the sound of grinding metal filled the air. A compartment opened on the robot's chest, and inside he removed his transmitter.

"I want to talk to Finn Foley."

Kraven smashed the window as Lincoln, Julep, and Finn raced to the door. Before they could get it open, the bug was on top of them, slashing at their clothes with his claws. In the struggle Finn wiggled out of his backpack and opened it, then dug around inside.

"You won't escape this time," the bug threatened.

Finn blasted him in the eyes with bug spray. The monster screamed in agony. Lincoln and Julep grabbed cans for themselves, and all three soaked the monster in the poison.

Kraven staggered around the room, destroying Ms. Applebaum's things. Framed photos fell to the floor, then a coffeepot. Even a mug that read *World's Greatest Assistant Principal* was smashed to pieces.

While he was blind, the kids ran into the hall with the bug screaming threats of revenge behind them.

"Little man?"

The voice was coming from Finn's pocket. He pulled the transmitter out of it as they dashed around the corner.

"Highbeam? How are you alive?" Finn cried. "I thought Kraven destroyed you."

"I'm a Class-One Demo-Bot with a full upgrade package," he said. "I have a repair app in case of catastrophic emergencies. Listen, we have a problem. Your mom found me in the—"

"We've got a bigger problem!" Lincoln shouted into the transmitter. "Kraven is here at school, and he's trying to kill us."

"Hang tight," the robot said. "I'm on my *zzzeeeck* way."

The kids rounded a corner but could still hear Kraven screeching.

"What do we do?" Lincoln asked.

"Find a place to hide until Highbeam shows up," Finn said, his heart pounding.

"There!" Julep said, leading them into an empty classroom. Finn closed the door, and the kids stood frozen in place.

"You might as well come out. You're going to die anyway. When my people come for this world, no one will survive!" Kraven bellowed, just as the classroom door flew off its hinges. The monster barreled through it, slamming into the opposite wall and staggering on his feet.

The kids ran out of the room and down the hall.

"You can't hide from me!" Kraven bellowed.

"We're going to try!" Lincoln said.

"I know a place. This way!" Julep said, making a sharp right that took them down a hallway.

"Where are we going?" Lincoln said as he looked over his shoulder.

"There!" Julep said, and she ran through the open door of the girls' bathroom. Once they were inside, Julep shut the door and turned off the lights.

Finn and Lincoln looked around in awe. They couldn't help themselves. The girls' bathroom was a place of legend. No boy had ever set foot inside its walls.

"There's a chair in here?" Lincoln said.

"And a mirror!" Finn cried.

"And soap!"

"They don't have that in the boys' bathroom?" Julep asked.

"No! They treat us like animals," Lincoln complained.

"Can we focus on the alien trying to kill us right now?" Julep asked. "If Highbeam doesn't get here in time, we need to think about a plan of attack."

An explosion filled the air.

"I have to confront him," Finn said.

"No you don't," Julep said.

"I can't hide in here," Finn said.

"Yes you can," Lincoln said.

"It's my fault he's here. If someone gets hurt because I was a coward, I'll never forgive myself. You don't have to come with me. You probably shouldn't, but I'm going out there to stop that thing," Finn said. He rushed back through the door.

"You're going to make me follow him, aren't you?" Lincoln asked Julep.

She nodded and dragged him back into the hall.

Kraven was in the auditorium. They could hear his angry voice all the way down the hall. He had a group of students with him. They whimpered every time he shouted.

"Where are you hiding the boy?"

"We don't know who you're talking about," a teacher cried.

"Liars! You're all liars," the bug roared.

"Are you sure about this?" Lincoln whispered to Finn.

"No, but I'm going to do it anyway," he said, stepping out into the open. Lincoln and Julep did the same. "I'm here!"

Kraven peered at him with his huge, empty eyes.

"I'm impressed, boy. I didn't expect you to have the courage to confront me," Kraven said, sneering.

"Let everyone go. I'm the one you want," Finn said.

"Very well. Go!"

Lincoln opened a set of double doors that led outside and gestured for the students and teachers to hurry through them. Soon the auditorium was empty.

"I will make you a deal, Earth boy," Kraven said as his wings extended. A moment later he was in the air, only to land with a thud in front of Finn. "Give me the weapon and I'll let your friends live."

Kraven took his shock blaster from the holster on his hip. He leveled it at Finn.

"But you are going to die," the bug promised.

Finn concentrated on opening a wormhole. He felt

the now-familiar rumble and heard the zipper slide aside. A whirlpool opened, and he and Kraven fell into it before the bug could react.

They came out of the tunnel several feet above the floor of the auditorium stage. The bug landed hard on its back with Finn on top of him. The air flew out of whatever the creepy thing called its lungs.

While Kraven recovered, Finn drove his shoulder into the bug's belly, then opened a second wormhole. He and the monster slipped into it and out into a hallway on the other side of the school. This time Kraven crashed hard against a wall.

Furious and desperate, the bug swung his tail and caught Finn's feet. He fell and Kraven pounced on him, pressing one of his hind legs onto the boy's chest. There was a hiss of burning flesh, and the bug yelped and yanked away. Finn looked down. Through his shirt he could see that the alien device was red-hot.

With Kraven distracted, Finn opened another wormhole, but before he could jump into it, the monster lunged forward and tackled him, sending them both through an open classroom door. Desks and chairs scattered in the fall. Books, homework, pencils, and sharpeners went in every direction. Finn also lost his hold on the lunchbox. It skittered just out of reach.

"This is over, Earth boy," Kraven hissed, wrapping both claws around his neck.

"Finn!" Julep cried as she and Lincoln raced into the room. "S'mores!"

What was she talking about? He was going to die and she was talking about food? Wait! *S'mores!*

With a free hand, Finn's fingers searched the floor until he found a pencil. It was perfect. All he needed was a crack in the locust's exoskeleton. Wait, was there something exposed under Kraven's rib cage, or was the lack of air in Finn's lungs making him see things? He couldn't be sure, but he was out of time. With all his strength he stabbed. The pencil slid between the armored plates and into the bug's gooey center. Kraven screeched and tumbled off him. While the monster rolled around on the floor, Finn retrieved the lunchbox, then he and Lincoln and Julep ran for their lives.

The police car radio squawked.

"We got a call from Ms. Applebaum at the elementary school," the dispatcher said with a laugh. "Guess who's down there? That's right, our new friend Mr. Grasshopper. This guy is all over town."

Deputy Day picked up the radio.

"Did you say grasshopper?"

"I did indeed," the dispatcher said. "We've gotten reports about him all weekend. Some dude in a costume, I guess."

Both deputies turned in their seats to eye Mr. Doogan.

"I told you," he said.

"We're on it!" Dortch shouted into the radio. Day flipped on the siren and steered toward the school. Seconds later they tore into the parking lot. Before they even stopped, the principal was trying to open the door.

"Brian, you have to stay in the car," Deputy Day said.

"You don't understand! One of my students is in trouble," he cried.

"And protecting him is our job," Deputy Dortch said. "Besides, you might scare more kids than help them the way you're dressed. Stay put. We'll take care of this!"

Before Doogan could argue, the deputies were out of the car and hurrying toward the school. Doogan watched through his window, hoping that they had arrived in time to avert a tragedy. As Dortch and Day stepped onto the lawn, the doors of the school opened and Finn Foley, Lincoln Sidana, and Julep Li raced outside. They seemed to be in a hurry to get somewhere and a second later the reason became clear. Sin Kraven barreled through the doors, screeching with rage.

Mr. Doogan had to do something. He clambered into the front seat. The deputies had left the keys in the ignition. He started the engine and put the squad car in drive. With his foot planted on the accelerator, he steered it forward, bouncing over the curb and tearing a path across the lawn, willing the car to go faster and faster. His palms lay on the horn just as he hit Sin Kraven head-on. The bug smacked against the windshield, bounced off, and then fell to the ground, either dead or unconscious.

Doogan got out of the car knowing he looked like a madman, but he didn't care. He was a principal. It was his job to keep his students safe. Kids gathered around him. They clapped and cheered.

Just then, Highbeam dropped out of the sky, landing on his feet in the center of the crowd. The clapping and cheering stopped. It was so quiet you could hear the wind whistle in the trees. Highbeam looked at the stunned crowd and cringed.

"Hey, Finn, if I shock everyone's brains, they will forget all of this, but there's gonna be a very long line for the bathroom."

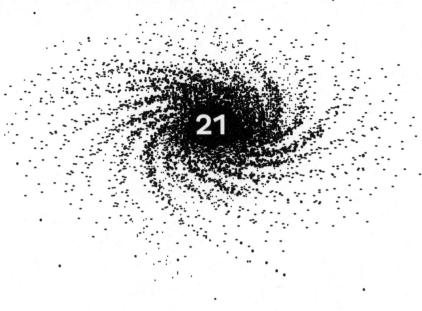

21

"**D**on't you dare!" Julep said. "People have a right to know the truth."

"You aren't going to stop the greatest toilet disaster in the history of this town, are you?" Lincoln cried.

Finn gave the robot a hug.

"It's good to see you, too, little man. Though it looks like you didn't need me."

"I did," Finn said. "I'm glad you're back. You're limping."

"Just a scratch. My upgrade will fix the rest in time." He pointed at Kraven. "Let's get this *zeeeck* critter back to Nemeth before he wakes up."

Finn held out the lunchbox but it was already bouncing.

"Uh-oh, something's coming through," Finn said.

"More bugs?" Julep asked.

"Everyone back up!" Highbeam shouted.

The zipper opened, and out of the lunchbox shot a small metal orb. It landed in the grass at their feet and a light flooded out of the top. Inside it was a holographic image of Dax. She was talking, but it was impossible to make out what she was saying. The recording was full of static.

"What is she trying to tell us?" Lincoln asked.

"Hard to say. The wormhole messes with technology," Highbeam said. "I guess we're going to have to ask her ourselves. Can you give it another try, little man?"

"Here we go," Finn said, concentrating.

As the wormhole appeared, Lincoln looked over and waved at the crowd of teachers and students who were watching everything in amazement. Then he and the others were sucked inside.

"Tell Ms. Applebaum we're sorry about her office," he said.

A few hurtling moments later, the group spilled onto the floor of the theater in Leah. As before, the oval windows above were occupied with unusual onlookers. An alarm sounded, and Commander Miles Teague, Ezekiel, and the bee girl entered.

"I will never get used to this," Julep said, taking more pictures with her phone.

"How come I'm the only one who gets sick?" Lincoln said after he bent over and barfed.

"Welcome back, Agent Highbeam," Commander Teague said, his voice booming in Finn's head.

"Here's your bug," the robot said. "His name is Major Sin Kraven. I suspect he has some useful information about the enemy."

The robot dropped Kraven to the floor. The creature let loose with a rant in a language Finn didn't understand. It was clear, though, that many of his words were not very nice.

"I'm hoping Pre'at has had some luck with the gizmo so we can send my buddy home without the stowaway on his chest. I'd also like to see Dax and my kids as soon as possible. Where is she?"

A door opened and Pre'at entered, leaving a trail of sweat behind her. In her hands was something hidden beneath a red cloth.

"Ah, the Earth children have returned, just in time to hear my big announcement," Pre'at said. "I've had a breakthrough with the wormhole generator."

"You figured out how to get it off me?" Finn asked hopefully.

"No. Not at all," she said. "I built a new one and added a few brilliant upgrades, if I do say so myself. My scans revealed that the original design had a few flaws. I increased the shielding to protect the technology. If it's pushed too hard, it could overheat and even explode. My version has none of those failings."

She removed the red cloth to reveal a perfect cube made from the same plastic-like material as the one on Finn's chest. There were even blinking lights swirling around inside it.

The aliens looking down on the meeting from above clapped and cheered from behind their windows. Teague looked pleased, and the bee woman buzzed happily around the room.

"Pre'at, your work will change the course of the war," Commander Teague said.

"Yay for you," Lincoln said, interrupting the celebration. "But what about the derp?"

"Pardon?"

"What about Finn?" he said. "We did everything you asked. We brought you the bug. We brought you the machine. You promised to take it off him when we came back."

Teague's mouth turned down.

"An opportunity arose that quite frankly could not be ignored. Building a new device required all our focus," Teague said.

"What opportunity?" Highbeam asked.

"Who are you to question the Commander?" Ezekiel

said. "We have all sworn allegiance to him. Where he leads, we follow."

"I swore allegiance to the Resistance," the robot said. "Not Teague."

"They are one and the same," the gorilla-man roared.

Lincoln nudged Finn. "Something's wrong," he whispered.

"Robot, please remain calm. All will be explained," Teague said to Highbeam, though he seemed offended that he had to do it. He gestured toward Kraven. "But first, would you be so kind as to help our guest to his feet."

"Our guest?"

Another door opened and through it came a dozen locusts. They marched with the confidence of people who felt at home in their surroundings. They gathered behind Teague, Ezekiel, and the bee girl in the center of the room.

"Today is a glorious day for the Resistance. We have signed a diplomatic agreement that ends our struggle with the Plague," Teague explained.

"What?" Highbeam cried.

Teague raised his hand to silence the angry crowd, then turned to the locust at the center of the others. He had white markings on his face, and a chest full of medals.

"Admiral Tan of the High Guard, it is my pleasure and duty as a symbol of our new friendship, and to satisfy the terms of our peace agreement, to offer this present to you and your people," he said.

Ezekiel snatched the cube from Pre'at's hands and gave it to the locust.

"How dare you!" Pre'at cried. "You can't give them that machine. They will destroy us all with it."

"The generator will end our conflict forever," Teague said to the aliens looking down from above. Many of them were booing him. The new partnership with the Plague had few supporters. "In exchange for this technology, the Plague has promised to leave our corner of the universe, never to return."

"Is that what they told you? And you believed them?" Highbeam shouted.

"I *believe* the lives of a hundred inhabited planets are worth a leap of faith," Teague said. "Agent Highbeam, I understand your distress. I know like many of us you risked much, and though our struggle was noble, it was also doomed. Eventually our weapons and resources would run out, and we would be of no use to the worlds we vowed to protect."

"And what of the worlds who aren't prepared for these filthy creatures?" Highbeam cried.

The locusts hissed at him and rubbed their back legs together.

Kraven managed to get to his feet without High-beam's help. He laughed loud enough for everyone to hear.

"Admiral Tan," he said, bowing with respect. "I am Major Sin Kraven. I request permission to speak."

"You have it," the locust said.

"I was the sole survivor of the disaster in Longdar City and witnessed the theft of the wormhole technology. Though I was wounded, I followed it to a planet called Earth, in a galaxy called the Milky Way.

"Earth is a fertile place, with almost limitless resources. The Plague could feast for a hundred years before it was spent. I have observed their people. They are simple, with few weapons that would concern us. They would stand no chance against us."

"Your heroism is noted and appreciated. Once our *gift* is installed in the mothership, you will lead the armada to Earth, *General* Kraven," Tan said.

Kraven bowed his head in respect, but Finn could see the satisfied expression on his face.

"What about Earth?" Finn asked. "We can't fight back!"

"We can't save everyone," Ezekiel said.

"General Kraven, report to the mothership," Admiral Tan said. "Prepare our people to leave this world and relay coordinates to Earth with the navigation center."

"It is my greatest honor," Kraven cried. He turned to

Finn and laughed. "Looks like I'll be seeing you again very soon."

"I believe we have made a lasting peace today," Teague said.

"You've just sentenced billions to death!" Highbeam shouted.

"That is enough, robot!" Ezekiel shouted.

"It's not nearly enough!" Highbeam roared.

Guards rushed inside to arrest him, but Highbeam fought back, knocking them across the room. The violence sent the chamber into chaos. The creatures above were pounding on their windows.

"I'll give you the same two choices I gave your partner," Teague said. "Accept this peace, or surrender and be imprisoned. I hope you are smarter than she was."

"Derp," Lincoln said, grabbing Finn's arm, "I'm only going to say this one more time. Take us home, now."

"He's right, Finn," Julep said. "These people are not our friends."

"But Highbeam—" Finn said.

"They're not his friends, either," Julep whispered.

Finn's mind rocked back and forth like a tiny boat on an angry sea. Nothing made sense anymore. Who were the good guys? Who were the villains? The Resistance was siding with the Plague? He reached up and placed his hand on the robot's arm, then gestured for Lincoln and Julep to do the same.

"Kid, don't you dare," Highbeam said, but it was too late. A wormhole opened beneath their feet, and a moment later the four of them crashed onto Finn's bedroom floor.

"Take me back!" Highbeam demanded. "My kids are there. My best friend is locked up in a cell."

"They'll destroy you, and I can't let that happen, again. I'll go get them for you," Finn said, just as his shirt caught fire. The machine underneath was as hot as the sun, and just as red. Finn tried to ignore it. He closed his eyes for a return trip, doing his best to focus. Unfortunately, no matter how hard he concentrated, nothing happened, not even the usual rumbling sound.

"Stop, Finn! It's overheating," Julep said.

Highbeam's face was at war with itself. It was impossible to read how he was feeling, but a loud, mechanical roar gave Finn a clue. The robot rushed to the bedroom window, opened it, and leaped outside.

"Highbeam!" Finn called after him. "Wait! Stay with us!"

"What just happened?" Julep said. "I thought he worked for the good guys."

"So did he," Lincoln said, shaking his head.

"What are we going to do now?" Finn asked his friends.

"I don't know," Lincoln answered, "but the world is in a whole lot of trouble."

22

Dax pounded on the force field that kept her locked in her cell. She demanded that someone set her free. The guards were ignoring her, but she didn't care. She would make them listen, somehow. They needed to know that Commander Teague had sold them out to the Plague. Giving the bugs a wormhole generator might get them off Nemeth's back, but it was just putting the suffering on another world.

"You're just going to let this happen?" she shouted. "Have you forgotten what it was like when they arrived? Have you forgotten how their pipelines inhaled all our water and the plants and even the minerals in the ground so we couldn't grow our own food anymore?"

No one answered. Defeated, Dax slumped against

the wall. They weren't listening. They believed in Teague so much they couldn't imagine he was wrong.

"This isn't why I joined the Resistance," she said to herself.

There was a *zap,* and several people cried out in pain. She heard bodies fall to the floor and the sound of weapons bouncing on stone. In the hall, shadowy figures were approaching. Her heart raced. Teague must have sent someone to shut her up permanently.

She braced for her death, only to see Pre'at appear outside her cell. Sweat was pouring down her face. "It's not why I joined, either," she said.

Dax watched the scientist open up a panel in the wall and fool with wiring. A moment later, the force field vanished, and she was free.

"Perhaps it's time to start our own resistance," Pre'at continued.

"I like how you're talking, but first we have to help Highbeam," Dax said.

"I assume you have a plan?" the scientist asked.

"Would you be nervous if I admitted I'm making this up as I go?"

"It would make me very nervous. That's why I brought help." She stepped aside, revealing a group of eight creatures Dax had never met but had seen peering down from windows in the chamber. They were the sole survivors of long-dead worlds.

"Wait! Pre'at, why are you helping me?" Dax asked warily.

"You can destroy my world, but you can't steal my inventions," Pre'at said. "My friends feel the same way."

"We've brought weapons," said two furry creatures that looked a bit like possums. They held hands and spoke in unison, as if they were sharing the same thoughts.

"We're going to give Earth a fighting chance. We have a ship in the shuttle bay. It can take us to there if you can find that rift you spoke about."

"I can find it," Dax said confidently.

An alarm blared and lights flashed in the hall.

"The guards know what we're doing. They're locking down the base. If we don't hurry, we won't be able to get out," one of the aliens said. He had the face of a lion.

"I'll meet you in the shuttle bay," Dax promised. "I need to pick up some kids."

23

Finn went into the bathroom to change out of his smoldering shirt. The heat from the machine had baked it black. His chest felt sunburned. It was the least of his worries.

The Plague was coming to Earth. Highbeam was a mess. The lunchbox was acting weird. The good guys were working with the bad guys. Nothing was going right, and no one knew how to fix anything. Finn imagined a life in a locust prison camp, watching everything around him turn to dust. And what would happen to his family—and his friends?

Lincoln, Julep, and Kate barged into his room.

"Those things are coming here. They're going to take over. We need to make a plan!" Kate cried. He could see she was panicked.

"Calm down, kid," Lincoln said.

"*No!* I'm not calming down. This is serious!" Kate stormed out of the room.

"She's right," Julep said. "We need to get to work."

"I'm not sure what we all think we can do," Lincoln said. "Unless you have a book in your backpack on how to stop the end of the world."

"Making fun of me is not helping," Julep said.

"I'm just saying that your dumb books about the Loch Ness Monster are not going to do us any good!"

"Those dumb books have helped keep us alive, Lincoln Sidana!" she shouted. "I think I should be with my family right now."

Julep stormed out of the room, just like Kate.

"This is dumb. What are a bunch of kids going to do against an invasion?" Lincoln said.

"Probably nothing," Finn snapped. "But being a jerk every time things get hard is probably not going to help, either."

Then, like the others, Lincoln stomped out of the room, leaving Finn alone. He sat on the floor and looked out the window. A million stars drifted lazily in the black sky. Tonight might be the last time he would look up at them without fear. How long would it take the Plague to attach the wormhole generator to their ship? How long before they were hovering in the sky?

Cold Spring was quiet. Mom was still not home. Kate kept her distance, locked inside her room. Finn reached out to both Julep and Lincoln, but they didn't take his calls. Highbeam ignored him every time he used the transmitter. He remembered a time not so long ago when he was done with people. He didn't need any of them. He couldn't count on them, anyway, but now . . . things had changed but once again he was abandoned.

Fine! He would find a way to stop the Plague by himself. How? He didn't have a clue, but something would come to him.

Without warning, the lunchbox hopped off his bedside table. A popping sound filled his ears, but it wasn't coming from the lunchbox. The noise was inside his shirt. He pulled it up and saw the device was lighting up like a spotlight. It all felt just like it had the night Kraven came to Earth. Something was coming through the lunchbox.

"What's happening?" Kate said as she rushed into his room.

"I'm not sure," he said as he rushed to his bedroom window. The sky was twisted into an ugly soup of black clouds and electricity. Lightning bolts ripped the night in two, and a swirling mass that looked like a giant amoeba rolled over the Earth. A terrible wind swept through the neighborhood, knocking down trees and telephone poles. Cars flew into the air like they were toys. Streetlights blinked off and on. Neighbors came out of their homes in robes and slippers to gawk at the strange weather.

"This is not good," Finn warned.

"Finn!" Mom's voice rang through the house.

"Up here!"

He heard Mom slam the front door and take the stairs two at a time. She hurried into his room and wrapped her arms around him.

"Are you okay? What happened at school? When did you get home? It's all over the news. What is that thing in the garage?" Kate drifted into the room, and Mom pulled her into the hug. "What do you know about this? Were you hurt? I don't understand a single thing that is going on." She pointed an angry finger at her kids. "Talk!" she commanded.

Finn sighed. He looked to Kate and gestured for her to spill the beans.

Kate took a breath. "My lunchbox opens shortcuts to other planets. A robot came out of it, then an evil giant bug. They're in a war, and the good guys needed the lunchbox to help win, but part of the machine that makes it work is stuck on Finn's chest. We tried to give it to them, but the robot's people wanted us to capture the bug."

"So we did," Finn said, taking over the explanation. "But when we went back to turn him over to them, we found out the good guys are working with the bad guys, and now they have their own machine that makes wormholes, and bugs are coming here to take over Earth."

Mom stared at them for a long time. Finn could almost hear her blink.

"Mom, are you okay?"

"Do you really expect me to believe that?" Mom cried.

In the window, a wormhole appeared above the house. It ripped open the sky, and from it came the Plague ship. It was bigger than anything Finn had ever seen, long and black, with a hull made from huge plates, not unlike the exoskeleton of the locusts inside it. Following behind were two smaller ships, though still incredibly massive.

Mom stared at it, stunned silent.

He and Kate left her in his room and hurried down the stairs and out onto the lawn. Neighbors were everywhere, staring up at the terrible ship with mouths open in shock. Dogs barked and raced around in a panic. Street lamps blinked on and off. Someone was crying from fear.

Finn reached into his pocket for Highbeam's transmitter. He held it to his mouth.

"I want to talk to Highbeam, Lincoln, and Julep," he said. "It's Finn. I know you're angry at each other. I know you're all angry at me, but the bugs are here and I don't know what to do, and I need your help."

As he stuffed the transmitter back into his pocket, Mom charged out of the house and grabbed him and his sister by the arms.

"We need to get back inside," she said.

"No, Mom," Finn said. "I might be the only person who can stop them."

"What a huge ego you've got, derp." Lincoln was the first to arrive. He came on his bike and huffed down the street. When he could finally speak, he pointed to the sky. "What's the plan?"

"The plan is to get in the car and drive away from here!" Mom tried to usher them toward the car just as a squad car screeched to a halt in front of their house. Deputy Day and Deputy Dortch leaped out. A moment later, Principal Doogan parked his Jeep nearby. His hand was in a cast and his face was covered in calamine lotion, but thankfully he was completely dressed.

"I'm assuming you two know something about this," Deputy Day said to Finn and Lincoln.

"Yeah, just tell us what to do," Officer Day said.

Julep's van stopped in the middle of the street, and she hopped out. Once again, Truman was behind the wheel.

"This is crazy!" he shouted to Finn.

"Go home and get Mom and Dad," Julep told him. "You need to get as far from here as you can."

"What about you?" he asked.

"My friends and I will handle this," she said with complete confidence.

He handed her a backpack through the window. It looked like it weighed more than her, and then he turned around and headed back the way he came.

"I brought as many books as I could," she confessed.

A sports car came up right behind her, and the driver slammed on the brakes. Dr. Sidana, Nadia, and Seth got out, all of them in a panic.

"Son, you have to come home with us right now!" Dr. Sidana told Lincoln.

"I need to be here with Finn and Julep," Lincoln said. "We might be able to stop that thing in the sky."

"Did you seriously just leave me out?" Kate cried.

"Sorry," Lincoln said. "And Kate. We all need to be here."

"Lincoln, this isn't open for negotiation!" Dr. Sidana said.

While Lincoln and his dad argued, Finn felt the

lunchbox shaking in his hand again. The sensation was similar to when the Plague ship arrived. He guessed something else was coming, though.

The lunchbox zipper slid aside and the lid flew open. Octopus arms of energy sprang out, twisting and twirling and scorching the lawn. A wormhole appeared, bigger than any his lunchbox ever created, and from it a spaceship appeared. It was silver and sleek, about the size of a bouncy castle and it crashed into the street, missing the squad car and Mr. Doogan's Jeep by inches.

"It's one of ours," a voice shouted, and Highbeam stepped out of the shadows. He had his weapons in his hand. "Though it's impossible to say if it's a friend or a foe. Teague may have sent soldiers to arrest me. They're going to wish they stayed home."

The hatch on the ship opened with a hiss. Steam rose out of it, and from inside stepped Dax Dargon.

"Big guy!" she said. "Are you ready to kick some bug butt?"

"Dax? How did you—where did you come from?"

"I'll explain later," she said, pointing to the sky. "Looks like they got here first. That's fine. I brought some friends to help us fight them."

Pre'at stepped out of the ship.

Highbeam looked furious.

"I was betrayed as well," Pre'at said. "A lot of us were."

From the ship came eight more figures, each more bizarre than the first.

"That woman is made of glass," Mom said incredulously. "And that one has a lion for a face. And that man is melting. And that one looks like a sponge."

Lincoln nudged Finn with his elbow.

"See, everyone does that when they see an alien," he said.

"Teague was wrong to join the Plague," the man with the lion face said. "He broke our hearts, but we're not going to stand for it. We've brought some of our worlds' most destructive weapons to help Earth and its people."

"We've got some pretty cool stuff," Pre'at said, patting a sack she had slung over her shoulder.

"It's not much, and it might not be enough, but it's the best we can do," Dax said. "Oh, and I almost forgot. Kids?"

A shiny, golden robot about half the size of Highbeam stepped out of the ship. Aside from his color, he looked a lot like Highbeam.

"Lugnut?" Highbeam cried.

"Dad!" The little robot hopped into Highbeam's arms and was followed by another robot, then another, and another and another, until there were twenty-five of them jumping around and grinning.

"Torque! Piston! Strut! Pump! What are you doing here?"

"Dax rescued us from the cranky man with eyes on his hands," Pump explained.

"He was creepy!" said Piston.

Another golden robot stepped out of the ship. She was nearly as tall as Highbeam and had a smile on her digital face.

"Goldplate?" Highbeam said.

"I see you're getting into trouble, Highbeam," she said. "Just like old times."

"Everyone, this is Goldplate. She's my . . . well, it's complicated."

"Doesn't look complicated," Kate said, teasing him with exaggerated kissing sounds.

"There's no time for a family reunion," Pre'at said. "The Plague will launch their feeding tubes once they're settled in the sky. We have to be ready. It will be the only time the ships will be vulnerable to an attack."

Finn stepped forward.

"What exactly are we going to do?"

Pre'at smiled.

"We're going to train all of you to fight," she said. "Welcome to the new Resistance."

The ship's arrival brought the police, military, and a number of weird people in black suits and sunglasses.

Pre'at used a device in her collection to create an invisible barrier to keep them out, allowing them to make plans without intrusion. Along with the eight alien beings, they gathered everyone together to show them the weapons they hoped would drive the Plague away. Pre'at scattered them on the lawn so everyone could get a good look.

A few of them looked silly, like a collection of weird toys, all blinking and making beeping noises. Some looked like bracelets. There were a couple of helmets and something that resembled a ping-pong paddle. Even when Highbeam added Kraven's huge weapon to the pile, Finn didn't think anything they had looked powerful enough to knock a spaceship out of the sky. Where were the obnoxiously huge video-game weapons? Where were the tanks? Where were the nuclear-powered missiles?

"Dibs on anything that shoots lasers!" Lincoln yelled.

"You're not really thinking about giving a weapon to a baby like Lincoln, are you?" Seth said as he pushed through the crowd. "Give it to me. I'm an athlete. I've got the best chance of doing some damage."

"Seth, cut the insults," Lincoln's dad said.

"Honey, he's right," Nadia said. "Seth is strong and quick on his feet. Lincoln is a little bit, you know . . ."

"I'd take one Lincoln over a million Seths any day," said Finn.

"What do you know?" Seth said.

"I know you suck," Finn said. "I know you get a weird thrill out of picking—"

"Finn, don't," Lincoln said.

"You're just like Chunky, all talk," Seth said. "That's why he gets underwear sandwiches every day. He's a loser, and so are you."

"Underwear sandwiches?" Bikram asked. He turned to his son. "What is he talking about?"

Lincoln's eyes locked on his shoes. "It's nothing."

Bikram turned to Seth. "Are you bullying my son?"

"Honey, boys will be boys," Nadia said. "It's good for a kid like Lincoln. Seth is toughening him up."

Bikram put his hand on Lincoln's shoulder.

"How long has this been going on?"

Lincoln shook his head. He still didn't want to tell his father the truth, even when it was obvious to everyone.

Dr. Sidana hugged Lincoln.

"I'm sorry, son," he whispered. Then he turned to Nadia and Seth. "Linc has never lied to me. I can always count on the truth from him, so something is happening that has changed him and I'm putting a stop to it right now."

"Bikram! You're blaming his bad behavior on us?" Nadia said.

"Please go home," Lincoln's father said to her. "If we somehow survive that thing in the sky, we're all going to have a very serious conversation."

"Bikram, what are you going to do?" Nadia asked.

"I'm going to help my son save the world."

24

"It's best to assign weapons to the person best suited to use them," Pre'at said. "Bolivar, would you like to start?"

A large green creature stepped through the crowd. He had a beak for a nose and an enormous shell on his back. It took him some time to get to the center of the group, and when he spoke his words were long and lazy.

"I am Bolivar, last survivor of the Tortoisian Collective. For this battle I offer my peoples' greatest weapon—the supersonic blast cannon. It fires a ball of sound energy so intense it has the destructive power of a meteor strike. It did great damage to the Plague mothership when it entered our atmosphere."

"Wow!" Finn said.

"How do you create something like that and still get conquered?" Mr. Doogan asked.

"My brothers and sisters were not known for our speed. The mothership was able to track our weapons and destroy them before we could fire again. Whoever uses it must stay on the move."

"We could do it," Deputy Day said, turning to her partner.

"If we mount it to the top of our squad car, we could speed through town and fire it over and over," Deputy Dortch said.

"You say it hurt the Plague ships? How? The ships are almost impenetrable. They're designed like a locust exoskeleton," Highbeam said.

"S'mores!" Julep cried.

"What's that, little lady?" Highbeam asked.

"The bugs have vulnerable places between the armor," Julep said with a hint of pride. "If you can get at it, you can really hurt them."

"That's some first-rate thinking, Ms. Julep," Highbeam said.

"When we were stationed on the mothership, we made a map," Dax said. "Maybe we can find some of those soft spots."

"Then it's settled. The deputies get the supersonic blast canon," Pre'at said. "Now, on to the inside of the ship. If we're going to do any serious damage to the bugs we need to know where to hit them. Dax, do you and Highbeam have any insider information?"

"You bet! There are three core control centers—the first being communications," Dax said. "Knocking it out is our best chance of causing chaos. You see, the bugs need instructions. If they don't get orders they have no idea what to do and all the orders come through the communication hub. If we control it, we will paralyze the whole ship—that means no one will fire weapons, no one will send out attack ships, and the invasion will come to a complete stop."

"Let's blow it up!" Lincoln said. "That one thing can save us all!"

"Unfortunately, no. We can't destroy it because if we do, a backup communication tower activates," Highbeam said.

"And another one after that, and another, and another," Dax said.

"So, if we don't destroy it then how do we stop it?" Bikram asked.

"We make it so that the bugs don't want to go near it and we have the answer right here, don't we, Cha-chara?" Pre'at said.

The man with the lion head stepped forward. He sniffed the air and licked his long fangs.

"I am the last leader of the pride of Eula Prime. My people developed this," he said, holding out a bag of something green and gooey. "It is a radiation gelatin we used to scare off the rhino mutants of the Xephyr Valley."

"It will eat through a containment suit," Pre'at said. "If we can get some into the communication center, the bugs won't dare go near it. It's dangerous, though."

"Then count me in," Dax said. "I've been in that room. I know the layout and I know how many bugs will be working."

"It's all yours. Break the seal, stick it on a flat surface, and get away as soon as possible." Pre'at handed Dax the green sack.

"The next core section is the engines," Highbeam said. "Once communications are down, no one will stand in our way, but disabling them won't be easy. There are eight of them."

"Wait! What about the two destroyers? Breaking the mothership is great, but they can still attack, right?" Deputy Day asked.

"What if you don't destroy the engines?" Mr. Doogan asked. "What if we use the mothership to ram the destroyers? It worked for me when I ran over Kraven. Why not his ship?"

"We could speed up the engines," Dr. Sidana said. "And *wham!* It's kind of genius."

"I love it," Highbeam said, "but changing the ship's speed is *zzzack* not as easy as pushing a button. The crew can slow the ship from the helm. If we want to stomp on the gas, we have to wreck the engines so they can't turn them off."

"Perhaps Carboni and Corlette can help," Pre'at said to the two furry creatures.

They pushed through the crowd, holding hands, and looked up into everyone's faces. Carboni, the one on the left, held out a golden glove.

"We are Tresilak," the creatures said in unison. "We create battle armor. Simple instructions. Put on wrist. Press button. Destroy!"

The creatures giggled.

"Let me see that," Lincoln said, and before anyone could stop him, he snatched it away and clicked it around his wrist. The metal glove liquefied and quickly leaked up his arm. It spread across his torso and legs like spilled milk until he was covered from head to toe in a massive robotic suit that made him three times his normal size.

"We've got a winner!" he shouted.

"Makes you strong. Makes you near invulnerable. Punch goes mega-boom!" the creatures said.

Lincoln stomped around, shadowboxing the air. "Wait until the kids at school see me!"

"This can't be a good idea," Julep said.

"I'm not sure a child can handle this," Pre'at said.

"Do you know how many people I've punched? This was made for me!" Lincoln cried.

"He's got a point," Finn said.

"I know we're all in trouble," Dr. Sidana said, "but I don't like the idea of my son running around an alien ship, even if he does have that suit. I know we're all desperate, but I won't let him go unless I'm by his side."

"I was hoping you might say that," Pre'at said as she slipped two silver bracelets around the man's wrists. "This is one of my brilliant creations. I know you will find them impressive. Clink them together."

Bikram did as he was asked and his hands lit up like bonfires. The energy coming off of them formed enormous, glowing knives with shining edges.

"I call them Alcherian scissors," Pre'at said. "They'll cut through anything—metal, rock, even Borchian Plasma Glass. They were intended for constructing subterranean bases. The blades are made from an ultra-high-frequency light. Impressive, right? Did I mention I invented them?"

Bikram clinked the bracelets together again, and they powered down.

"You can use them to destroy the regulators that control engine speed," Highbeam said. "I'll tell you everything you need to know later."

"All right, well, we have plans for two of the three stations. What's next?" Kate asked.

"Ship's guidance," Highbeam said. "Mr. Doogan's plan to slam the mothership into the others is a good one, but it means someone is going to have to take the wheel."

Finn was about to step forward to volunteer when he felt his mother's hand on his shoulder. She pulled him and Kate out of the crowd and knelt down beside them.

"Don't even think about it," she said. "You two are not volunteering for this. Let the others do the dangerous stuff. We can stay down here and help."

"Mom? We can't just watch," Kate said. "A unicorn would never wait for others to be courageous."

"You are not a unicorn!"

Without warning, the ground buckled and rocked. Everyone tumbled about as houses shook. Car alarms cried in protest. Dogs howled.

"Was that an earthquake?" Dr. Sidana asked.

"No! Look!" Mom said, pointing down the street. A massive tube fell from the sky and drilled into a neighborhood several blocks away. It snaked up to the mothership hovering miles above the ground.

"That's a feeler," Dax explained. "It's searching for the best places to plant a feeding spike. Once it finds the right spot, the ship will launch them all over the planet. It happened on Nemeth when I was a little girl."

"Everyone, get some rest. The spikes will launch in the next few hours. We have to be ready," Pre'at said.

"Kid, can you help me with something?" Highbeam asked Finn.

"I missed part of the plan when I was talking to my mom," Finn said. "I should probably find out what it was."

"I'll catch you up," Highbeam promised. "Right now, I *zzzack* need your help with something." He left his children with Goldplate and Dax, then led Finn into the garage. Once the door was closed, he handed the boy a small cloth bag. Finn turned it over in his hand and a screw fell out.

"What's this?" he asked.

"It's a J-23—the part lost in the wormhole. Dax brought me a new one."

"This is what's been causing the glitches?" Finn asked.

Highbeam nodded. "And why my repair app isn't working as well as it should."

"So are you saying you have a screw loose?"

Highbeam's digital face became a sour frown.

"Hardy-har-har. *Zzzzack!*"

"What do you want me to do?" Finn asked.

Highbeam sat down on the floor and turned away

from Finn. The back of his head opened, revealing a knot of wires and glowing tubes.

"I want you to fix me," he said.

"What if I break something?" Finn asked. "What if I make you worse?"

"Have a little faith in yourself, kid," Highbeam said.

Finn snatched a screwdriver and peered into the maze of circuits to get a better look. There were so many parts inside Highbeam's head, he couldn't find a place for the screw to go. The screwdriver wasn't helping, so he probed with his finger. Way in the back he felt a hole. It was deep inside and it would be hard to get to, but not impossible.

"You know, I was thinking that if you wanted to try, this would be the time to do it," the robot continued.

"Try what?"

"Finding your dad."

"I tried, Highbeam," Finn admitted. "I used the transmitter and the generator. It took me somewhere strange. There was a man, and he . . . it's hard to explain. I'm not sure I even understand, but I think going there is why the machine keeps overheating, now. I think I broke it and it was all for nothing."

"Nothing?"

"I don't think I want to see him. He left and didn't come back. Maybe that's all I really need to know."

"I've been around long enough to know a thing or

two, and the truth is that folks spend too much time thinking about what they don't have, and they completely ignore what they've got. Like your mom, and your sister *zzzeeeck*, and Lincoln—"

"Lincoln?"

"This is going to come as a surprise, but kid, he's your best friend. And you've got Julep. Plus, you've got me. I know all of us can't replace your dad, but if you ask me, you've got more family than you need."

"This conversation smells a lot like one of those times when I'm supposed to learn something," Finn said.

Highbeam laughed.

"For a man made of metal I'm pretty transparent."

"Just a second." Finn's fingers eased the screw into the hole, then gave it a few turns with the screwdriver until it was tight. He heard a soft hum come from inside the robot's head. "That's it. How does it feel?"

Highbeam stood and Finn watched all the parts of his body turning and adjusting. The dents from his fight with Kraven pounded themselves out until they were smooth and shiny. Soon there wasn't a scratch on him. He gave himself a few stretches, then a good shake, and his face lit up with digital fireworks.

"Little man, I feel like I just got a factory reset!" He danced a little jig, and they both laughed. "Best of all, I can get rid of these clothes!"

Highbeam ripped off the shorts and the T-shirt, shredding them in two with one swift yank.

"I have to say," Finn said, "naked Highbeam is going to take some getting used to."

"Last chance, buddy," the robot said, tapping Finn's chest lightly. "You can go see him. I'll go with you. It might turn out good, might turn out bad, but at least you would know."

Finn gazed out the window. All his friends and family were in the yard outside, working together, preparing for the fight of their lives.

"No, I'm okay with my glitch."

Highbeam's face turned into a question mark.

"I'll explain later," Finn said. "We've got work to do."

25

When the sun peeked over the horizon, everyone gathered. Pre'at went over the plan once again, while Highbeam projected a three-dimensional map out of his face. It showed each section of the mothership and the places the heroes would attack, along with some video he had taken from his and Dax's time on the ship as spies. They went through each person's responsibilities. Finn learned that with the help of another weird weapon, Mr. Doogan had volunteered to take control of steering the ship, and that even Julep would be going up there to cause some trouble. Finn's job was to open wormholes and get everyone where they needed to be and back again. It made him nervous. He wasn't sure the machine could do it now that it was broken, but he kept that to himself. He didn't want to worry the others.

"Where's Kate?" he asked when he noticed his sister was not with the group.

"She's upstairs getting ready," Mom said. "Whatever that means."

Finn found her in her room, watching her once-favorite show, *Unicorn Magic.*

"What are you doing?"

"Getting inspired," she said.

"Did Pre'at give you a job?" he asked.

She grinned. "Yep! An awesome one."

Before he could ask her to explain, a loud droning boom filled the air.

"What's that?" she asked.

"They must be releasing the feeding spikes." Finn grabbed her hand. "C'mon!"

"It's time," Highbeam said when everyone gathered in the yard.

Finn stepped forward with the pink unicorn lunchbox in his hand. Lincoln and Julep joined him, their faces a combination of determination and worry.

"Finn, are you ready?" Mr. Doogan asked.

"He's ready," Highbeam said.

"Just a little advice, derp," Lincoln said to Finn. "Now is not the time to worry about getting in trouble."

"All right, deputies," Pre'at said. "Get to your vehicle. Be careful, and remember to give the cannon a few seconds after each shot. It allows the device to realign. If not, well, the kickback will flatten your car."

"We understand. Good luck," Deputy Day shouted to everyone. She and Deputy Dortch raced to their squad car. Finn watched them drive through an opening in the barrier with their sirens filling the air.

"As soon as they fire the first shot, we attack," Highbeam explained, but he barely had time to finish when they heard a loud *WHOMP!* A white comet streaked into the sky, screaming against the wind until it crashed into the bottom of the mothership. There was a huge explosion, and when debris fell to the ground, everyone cheered. A gaping hole was revealed, giving everyone a boost of confidence, even if the ship was still intact.

A faint alarm could be heard from above, and then a glowing blue laser shot down from the ship. It crashed into a neighborhood several blocks away, causing a sonic boom that shattered every car window on Finn's street.

"They're firing back! All right, Finn, let's do this," Highbeam said.

"Please be careful," Mom begged. She hugged him tight.

"And don't die," Kate said.

"I'll do my best," Finn promised.

Goldplate and the twenty-five kid robots gathered around, as did Julep. She put on a strange pair of goggles.

"What are those?" he asked.

"They told me they're called imagination projectors," she said.

Finn closed his eyes and heard the rumbling start. The lunchbox jerked and a hole appeared beneath them, made of space itself. The robot kids leaped in like they were cannonballing into a pool. Highbeam and Goldplate followed, then Julep, and finally Finn. In the blink of an eye they reappeared inside a dark, hot hallway in the mothership. The clicking of legs rubbing together smashed their eardrums, and a sour smell invaded their noses.

"Why is it so hot?" Julep asked.

"It matches the climate of their planet," Highbeam explained. "Guards are coming. Quiet!"

Everyone stayed still as statues until the guards moved farther down the hall.

"Okay, little lady. Let's put the magic goggles to work," Highbeam said.

"What do they do?" Finn asked. He had missed their explanation entirely and only knew they came from the creature who called himself 4.59. He was a brain in a floating jar of liquid.

"It was developed by the Montoo. It makes anything I can imagine comes to life."

"No way!" Finn said.

"Yes way!" Julep said as she swung her backpack off her shoulders. Inside she found a book about Bigfoot. "And as you know, I've got an awfully big imagination."

Suddenly, a monster appeared in the hall. It was covered in matted white fur and had a mouth full of broken teeth. It was so large, it pushed everyone against the walls.

"RRRRRRR!"

"Is that a Bigfoot?" Finn cried.

"It is, and I think he needs some friends!" Julep said happily. She closed her eyes, and in a flash the space was filled with dozens of hairy, ferocious Bigfoots. They arrived just in time. Doors opened at either end of the hall and bug soldiers charged in with weapons drawn.

"Go, kid, we've got this," Highbeam said to Finn. "Come back later and pick us up."

"We're gonna have some fun breaking stuff!" Goldplate cheered. "Demo-mode!"

"Demo-mode!" the robot kids echoed. Their heads sank below their shoulders. Their arms whipped into a frenzy, spinning like windmills, and they ran forward, plowing through the approaching locust soldiers.

Julep's army of Bigfoots joined the fight, howling and shrieking.

"Be careful, Finn Foley!" Julep said as she imagined a lurching pack of undead zombies into the fight. The smile on her face gave him butterflies.

A second later he was falling through another wormhole that emptied out into his yard. He landed with a thud. *Oof!* Then he caught a face full of water. His mom and Kate were spraying him with the garden hose.

"What are you doing?" he cried.

"This is our job," Kate explained.

"Pre'at is worried the machine on your chest will overheat, so we're going to cool you down each time you use it," Mom said.

"Best. Job. Ever," Kate said.

He waved them off and got to his feet.

"They're up there," Finn said to everyone as he shook water out of his ears.

"My turn." Dax stepped forward with the radiation gelatin pack in her hands. She had a video camera mounted to her head and several strange gadgets hanging from her pants.

"What's with all the stuff?"

"Pre'at wants me to document every second I'm in the wormhole," she said. "Do you need to take a look at the map again so you know where the communication center is?"

"No, all I really have to do is focus on where I want to go," Finn said. "The machine does the rest."

A second later he proved it to her when they appeared in the communication room. Their sudden arrival surprised the five locusts working there, but not for long. They leaped into the air and flew at Dax and Finn with their claws ready.

Finn ducked as Dax fired her shocker, knocking each bug to the ground one by one. With nothing to stop them, she cracked the radiation gelatin pack in two and slapped the pieces onto the wall. A hissing gas quickly escaped from it and spread across the room.

"Let's go." Finn took her hand, and in a flash they were back in his yard. This time they both suffered the garden hose assault.

"The engine room is next!" Pre'at shouted.

"Not if I drown," he cried.

Lincoln slipped on his glove and his father activated his light knives. "We're ready!" Lincoln said. "Dad, would it be cool if I had a talk with Seth while I'm wearing this?"

"Let's focus on the alien monsters first," Bikram said.

Finn concentrated on the map of the mothership.

The engines were in the lowest deck. Once he could see them in his head, a wormhole appeared. Lincoln and his father dove in and Finn followed, only to come out on a catwalk high above eight immense and noisy machines. It was the hottest place on the ship so far. Alarms shook the air.

"Don't throw up in the suit. Don't throw up in the suit!" Lincoln chanted to himself.

"What's with the sirens?" Bikram shouted. "I thought you and Dax shut off communications."

"I don't know!" Finn cried.

"All right, well, let's hurry."

"Halt!" A gang of locust soldiers raced toward them. One fired a sonic blast that missed Finn's head by inches. It crashed into the catwalk and the floor buckled. The trio held the railing to keep from falling over the side.

"I've got this." Lincoln brought his fists down hard on the catwalk. The impact sent a ripple through the steel girders, and the locusts were flung to the floor below. Unfortunately, the damage to the walkway caused everything to sway wildly back and forth.

"My bad," Lincoln said.

The platform fell, sending them plummeting into the abyss.

26

Finn held the lunchbox tight and shouted for a wormhole to appear. Much to his surprise, one did, directly beneath them, and in midair. Lincoln, his dad, and Finn sank into it and came out from another one that opened mere inches from the floor. The landing was harsh, but they were alive.

"Okay, what's important is no one got hurt," Lincoln said when they got to their feet.

"You are so grounded," his dad said.

The machine sizzled under Finn's shirt. Some of the lights inside it popped and died.

"What's wrong with that thing?" Lincoln said.

"It's nothing. Just hurry. I'm supposed to take you two right back and pick up Mr. Doogan."

"Hold your horses," Lincoln said, and he and his

father went to work smashing the engine exactly the way Pre'at and Highbeam told them to. While Finn watched, another wormhole opened behind him, one he didn't ask for, and he fell through it, landing on his back in the yard.

Kate and Mom squirted him with the garden hose. This time it was welcome.

"Honey, you don't look good," Mom said.

"I'll be fine," he told her. "Pre'at, the generator activated all by itself. It sent me back here. Lincoln and his dad are still in the engine room."

Pre'at lifted Finn's shirt to look at the machine. She couldn't hide the worry in any of her eyes.

"This isn't good. Listen, the plan is timed perfectly. You can go back for your friends, but not until the job is done. Right now, let's worry about getting Mr. Doogan into the navigation center. Can you do it?"

Finn nodded, and Pre'at helped him stand.

"No unnecessary jumps from now on," she whispered into his ear. It was obvious she didn't want Dax or any of the others to hear her. "The generator is about to die. Every wormhole it opens has to count."

He nodded.

"I'm ready," Mr. Doogan said as he slipped a helmet on to his head. "Let's go carjack an alien spaceship."

Another blast hit the bottom of the mothership, causing more damage. The deputies were at it again.

The principal put his hand on Finn's shoulder, and a second later they were sliding into the navigation room. A locust soldier was hunched over a console. He didn't notice their arrival.

"This is navigation to the engine room," the bug shouted into a communicator. "The ship is accelerating on its own!"

Finn smiled. Lincoln and Dr. Sidana had done their jobs.

No one answered the bug, and he slammed his arm down on the console, breaking the communicator.

"What is going on here?" he screeched, then spun around to leave, only to come face to face with Mr. Doogan and Finn.

Finn gasped. The bug was Sin Kraven.

"You! This is your fault, isn't it?"

"With a little help from some friends, like the good people of Xenia who lent this to me," the principal said as he pointed to his helmet. "It's called the Ex Machina. It lets me take control of machines, even very big spaceships filled with creepy crawlies."

A steering wheel made of light appeared in front of the principal. He put his hands on it and gave it a sudden turn. There was a terrible collision, and he,

Finn, and Kraven flew off their feet. Outside the door, screams rang out, then huge explosions. Everything started to shake.

"What are you doing?" Kraven shouted.

Doogan turned the wheel sharply to the left, and another shocking impact tossed them around again. Kraven staggered to his feet. There was murder in his empty black eyes. Mr. Doogan braced for an attack, but instead, the bug darted toward the door.

"He's going to warn the others!" Finn shouted.

"I have a feeling they already know," the principal replied.

Finn fished Highbeam's transmitter out of his pocket.

"Lincoln?"

"Dude, we did it!" Lincoln's voice was perfectly clear. He was loud and excited as he shouted over the noise of the busted engines. "Where did you go?"

"Sorry. The generator is acting weird. I'm with Mr. Doogan, and we just crashed the mothership into the destroyers."

"Duh!" Lincoln shouted. "We sort of noticed when we were flung to the other side of the room."

"We've got a problem. Kraven knows what we're doing, which means he's probably heading toward the ship's wormhole machine. If he gets it, he could open a new tunnel and move the ship to safety. We have to stop him."

Highbeam's voice cut in. "Everyone head to the front of the ship. That's the most likely place for the bugs to install the generator. Finn, go home. We'll call you when we need you. Right now it's too dangerous for you to be here."

Finn focused on home and leaped into the whirlpool that appeared. When he skidded onto the grass, Mom and Kate were there with the hose. If they hadn't been ready, Finn was sure his clothes would have caught on fire.

"I don't know how many more times I can do this," Finn said to Pre'at.

"Something's wrong," Pre'at said, completely ignoring him. She was holding a pair of binoculars to one set of eyes.

"What now?"

She handed Finn the binoculars, and he focused on the the mothership just in time to see it smash into a destroyer. *BOOOOOOOOOM!* There was a massive explosion. Fire leaped out of the ship and into the sky.

Mr. Doogan was still causing havoc.

"This is what we wanted to happen," Finn said. "Right?"

Pre'at frowned. "Do you see those black shuttles circling the mothership?"

Finn strained his eyes until three tiny ships came into focus. They were zipping around the front of the massive vessel, firing their weapons at a tower.

"What are they doing?" he asked.

"They're destroying their own communication hub so the backup will take control. When that happens, they'll be able to talk to one another again." Tiny balls of fire bloomed every time they zipped by.

"If that happens, they can order a ground attack," Pre'at continued. "They'll come in the thousands. We won't be able to fight them."

"They'll come down here?" Kate asked.

Finn kept watching the ship. He saw a massive fireball, and when the smoke cleared, the communication tower was gone.

"They've done it," he said.

"The communication hub is back online. They'll launch a ground attack now!" Pre'at shouted to the others, before turning back to Finn. "Go get your friends. We did our best, but it's time to retreat."

Retreat. He couldn't believe it. They were so close to winning!

Finn closed his eyes to activate a tunnel, but something on his chest popped. The lunchbox lid opened and belched smoke. He heard crackling under his shirt. He lifted it and saw the machine on his skin was no longer transparent. It was murky and gray. The lights inside it were sputtering and drowning in some kind of gas.

"I'm sorry. I think it's busted."

27

"Can you fix it?" Finn cried. He was lying on a work-bench in his garage as the scientist poked and prodded him. The aliens gathered and watched.

Pre'at didn't have to say *Of course I can fix it.* Her face was shouting it at him.

"Hand me that wrench" was her only reply.

Her work seemed achingly slow to Finn. His transmitter was open, and he could hear his friends, shouting for him to rescue them. He heard explosions and angry voices. Lincoln cried out in pain. Mr. Doogan fought attackers, but it was clear they were outnumbered.

A familiar and menacing voice rang out from the transmitter.

"You have failed, Earth boy," Kraven said with a

wicked laugh. "Our soldiers will be on the ground in seconds. There is nowhere you can hide."

They heard the clicking of back legs, and then the transmission went dead. Finn tried to activate it again, but no one responded.

Pre'at didn't give up, but by the time she got the machine working, an hour had passed without so much as a peep.

"I'm going to be honest with you," Pre'at said. "What I've done to this machine is a temporary fix. It won't last much longer—maybe two or three times at most. I suspect it will also be tremendously painful each time you use it. I know you want to save your friends, but the odds that any of them are still alive are slim. I am encouraging you to go into your house and pack what you can carry, then use the machine to find another world, one that's safe for you and your family. You will be a wanted criminal almost everywhere you go. The Plague will chase you if they can, but you will be alive."

"We can't leave Earth," Mom said. "Everything is here."

"You don't have a choice."

Mom and Kate helped Finn into the house.

"The suitcases are in my bedroom closet. Pack only what you need—clothes, good shoes, socks. We need medicine, everything in the cabinet, and toothbrushes, and get that first-aid kit from under the bathroom sink," Mom said. Finn could tell she was trying to sound strong, even though she looked gray and frightened.

Finn and Kate did as they were told, going into their own rooms to gather the things they thought they would need. It wasn't long before Kate returned with her laptop.

"Look at this," she said, turning the screen in his direction. She was watching a video of locusts flying out of the massive ship. There were so many, they blocked out the stars. They landed in the streets of Cold Spring with their weapons ready. People screamed and ran in panic. "It's really happening. It's the end of the world."

Finn sat her down on his bed.

"There has to be something we can do!" she said.

"If I knew how to fix this, I would!" Finn said.

"I have an idea." Kate said. She typed something into the search menu on her computer, and the screen flooded with images from the show *Unicorn Magic.* "Let's talk to them!"

"Huh?"

"The unicorns! Highbeam said they were warriors. They will help us."

"Kate, you're being silly!"

"I'm not being silly!" Kate's lip wobbled. "Summerstream says it's never over if there is still hope. What do we have to lose?"

"Uh . . . our lives? The lunchbox can't make too many

more wormholes, Kate. If I waste one a trip to see a bunch of horses with horns on their heads, we might be stuck here with the Plague. We need it to get to safety."

"They'll listen to me, Finn," Kate said. "C'mon! Everybody helped. All I did was turn the hose on you. This is how I can make a difference!"

Finn dropped his head into his hands. He was so tired and dizzy. He had lost his friends and now his home. He was about to stand and walk away when he remembered something the strange old man said to him.

Listen to your sister! Her idea might save the world!

A dazzling world of one-horned horses appeared in his thoughts and the name Haven appeared in his mind. If his sister's plan didn't work, Haven might be the perfect place to start over. Either way, it was worth a shot.

"All right, let's do it." He squeezed Kate's hand and closed his eyes.

They soared across the universe. Finn's chest felt as if he had fallen into a volcano. He was barely conscious when they landed in a meadow of gold and green grass. The sky above was crystal blue, and a gorgeous rainbow arched in the sky. Fluffy clouds floated overhead. It was just like the picture on Kate's lunchbox. Finn lay still, trying to catch his breath as the pain slowly eased.

"Are you okay?" Kate asked. She held his hand tight, as if hoping to lend him some of her strength.

"I'm starting to feel better," he said as he sat up. "Kate, this might be the place. I think we could all be safe here."

"Look!" his sister cried.

In the distance he saw them—a herd of pastel-colored beasts with wild creamy manes in impossible hues. They lifted their heads, huffed as if bored, and went back to munching on the grass.

Kate squealed and rushed toward them. Finn chased after her, but he was so tired he couldn't catch up. Moments later they were within inches of a silver unicorn with a pink horn.

"She looks just like Moondancer," Kate murmured as she held out her hand. The unicorn ignored her. "Um, my name is Kate Foley. My planet is under attack. My friends and family fought back, but we failed. On Earth, everyone knows unicorns are magical and brave. I have learned a lot from you, and now I need your help."

She held up her brother's hand so the unicorns could see the lunchbox.

The unicorn was silent and continued eating. It dawned on Finn that maybe it wasn't a magical and intelligent creature like the ones on *Unicorn Magic.*

"C'mon," Finn said, tugging his sister's arm. "It's

just a dumb horse. This was a waste of time. Let's go home. We'll bring everyone here. We'll be safe."

Kate tried to shake him off, but he pulled her along, back through the field.

"No! They're different. They're special!"

When the unicorns were no longer in sight, Finn lifted his shirt, hoping the cool air might lower the temperature of the generator. He needed to give it a few seconds before he used it again.

"I can't believe it," Kate said, her voice strangled and defeated. "I was so stupid! I wasted all that time watching that dumb show and eating the cereal and buying the books and it was all for nothing! Unicorns are stupid!"

The sound of beating hooves filled their ears. The silver unicorn appeared behind them.

"It probably wants you to give it an apple," Finn said.

"I have no need of an apple," the unicorn said.

"It talks!" Kate squealed.

"What do they call the beings that invaded your planet?"

"The Plague," Finn said.

The unicorn let out a loud whinny. "These villains have destroyed many worlds. Our former masters tried to rid the universe of them, but they also failed," the unicorn said.

"See! I told you," Kate cried. "They're just like the show. Is your name Skydancer?"

"No, child. My name is Blood Reaper, son of Goremonger, from the Merciless Herd."

"It's not exactly like the show," Finn said under his breath.

"I command ten thousand strong, and we are at your service."

A stampede of unicorns charged toward them and gathered around the kids. It was hard to reconcile their adorable features with the savagery Highbeam had described, but Kate was right. Maybe they could help.

Finn told them his plan, which involved a lot of poking bugs with horns. It seemed to satisfy Blood Reaper and his mate, Deathkick. Blood Reaper offered his back to Kate, and Deathkick did the same for Finn. Once they were mounted and ready, Finn held the lunchbox tight. He focused on Cold Spring, and a wormhole opened. Like before, he was overcome by pain. The machine was lightning-bolt hot now and felt like it was tearing him apart. While thousands and thousands of unicorns charged through the tunnel, a thunderous stampede of fury, Finn used all his strength just to stay on Deathkick's back.

When they arrived in his front yard, there were bugs everywhere, firing their weapons and terrorizing people. The soldiers and police officers that filled the streets were not ready for the Plague's advanced weapons, but the second the unicorns appeared, everything changed. Finn and Kate galloped into the fight, their unicorns impaling locusts with ease. The bug exoskeletons were no problem for the sharp horns. Blood Reaper earned his name many, many times over in the carnage, as did Deathkick. It was exactly what Finn's team needed to push back the invasion, even if he and his sister shared a number of nauseous looks.

"This is a lot grosser than I thought it would be," Kate admitted.

With the unicorns and the bugs fighting to a frenzy, he begged Deathkick to let him off. The generator was still working, even if the edges were now dead and black. He still had a chance to save his family and what was left of the team. He helped his sister down from Blood Reaper, and they raced through the deadly fight to rejoin the team. His mother was waiting with open arms. She pulled him tight and held him there.

"Kate and I found a place to hide. I think we'll be safe there."

"Then we should go now," Pre'at said. "These creatures you brought are making a difference, but I do not believe it will be enough."

Finn nodded. It was time to admit they had failed.

Mom and the aliens gathered close. Kate reached

for Finn's free hand and gave it a squeeze. Finn closed his eyes to concentrate one more time, recalling the green fields and the blue sky of Haven. But just before the rumbling began, the transmitter in his pocket vibrated, and a single voice shouted to him across space.

"DERP!"

Finn snatched it from his pocket and raised it to his mouth.

"Lincoln! You're alive!"

"We're all alive, dude, but not for long. The bugs have locked us up in some kind of detention facility."

"It's on the eighth floor," Highbeam shouted.

"Come get us! We have to stop Kraven! He's going after the other wormhole generator," Julep said.

Finn looked to the others. "I can't leave them behind!"

Pre'at looked as if she wanted to argue with him, but then all of her eyes softened.

"Go."

"Go!" Mom cried. "Go get your friends!"

Finn was crippled with searing pain when the whirlpool appeared. He fell to his knees, and the others had to help him stand. The machine was dying, and it was taking Finn with it. With the help of his mom and Kate, he got to his feet. Dax wrapped an arm around his shoulder, and together they stepped into the tunnel and came out in a dark hallway on the mothership.

There were fires everywhere, and sirens were blasting his ears. Bug soldiers raced past them in a panic. Finn was sure they noticed Dax and him, but they were too concerned with saving their own lives to do anything about the invaders.

Dax leaned him against the wall until he got his bearings. "This is going to be okay, Finn," she said. "We just do this one step at a time."

Finn nodded. He heard a cracking sound from beneath his shirt. He lifted it and watched the strange object on his chest turn black. All the little lights inside were snuffed out, and without warning the entire thing crumbled to dust and fell to the floor. The lunchbox lid opened and flame shot out, then thick black smoke.

"How will we get them home?" Finn said.

"Let's just focus on finding them first," Dax said.

Together, they made their way toward a door with a flashing red sign above it. When Dax pressed a green pad, the door slid open. Inside, he saw Mr. Doogan standing behind a strange, shimmering barrier.

"Dax! Finn!" the principal cried. "Finn, you look terrible."

Dax pressed another pad on a nearby wall, and the barrier vanished. Just in time for Doogan to catch Finn as he fell to the floor.

"Where are the others?" Finn gasped as Doogan held him up.

"They took them this way," the principal said as he steered the boy and Dax through another doorway. There they found Lincoln and his dad, Julep, and Highbeam and his family.

"Dude! They took my armor!" Lincoln complained when Dax shut down their barrier.

"They took all the weapons," Dr. Sidana said.

"Finn, you look terrible." Julep took his other arm to help Dax carry him along.

"I feel terrible," Finn admitted.

"Can you walk? We have to stop Kraven," Highbeam said.

"He'll make it," Dax said. "He's tough."

It was a miracle he was still standing, but Finn didn't disagree. Highbeam lifted him into his arms to carry him, and together, the team ran down the hall as explosions rocked them from every side. The ship was falling apart around them.

"Don't worry, kid. We're not far," Highbeam promised.

Finn was in so much pain he wasn't sure what was real anymore. He looked up into the robot's face and saw his father's eyes looking back at him. For a moment he thought he had gone back in time, to when he had fallen off his bike and twisted his ankle and his dad carried him all the way home. Even his surroundings felt strange to him—up was down and left was right. Everything was like a series of photographs flashing in his eyes, and he only caught snippets of what was happening. The hallway passed by so fast. There was a door Highbeam and his kids kicked down, then a brightly lit room with some kind of machine in the center. Kraven was hovering over it.

"Not this guy again," Highbeam said, snapping Finn back to reality. Kraven was standing between them and the second wormhole cube, pecking coordinates into its keypad.

"Stay back," he hissed.

"Not likely," Highbeam said. He set Finn down on the floor, and the robot charged at the bug. They traded vicious punches, tossing each other from one end of the room to the other. This time they were evenly matched, but when Goldplate and the robot kids jumped into the fight, Kraven was outnumbered.

Still, Finn knew how cunning the bug could be. At any moment Kraven could get the upper hand. Finn wouldn't underestimate him again.

"Help me get to the generator," Finn said to his friends.

"Finn, that's a terrible idea. Let someone else do it," Bikram said.

"I know how it works," Finn said.

Julep wrapped her arm around him, and Lincoln did the same. Together, the trio pushed through the smoke and fire while the bug and robots battled. It seemed like a million miles away to Finn. When they finally reached it, they held him up as he eyed the keypad.

"Are you going to take us home?" Lincoln said.

"Not yet," Finn said as he used the keypad and screen to scroll through planets. Each world that appeared was populated. He couldn't send the Plague where they could terrorize another civilization, but was there a place in the universe where they couldn't hurt anyone else? He kept looking, but there was nowhere safe to send them. Nowhere!

Nowhere.

That was it! He frantically typed 000000 into the keypad, a number that didn't match with any world in the database, and he pressed the green button. The cube lit up like a sun, and outside an enormous wormhole appeared. It swallowed the two crumbling destroyers, and finally the mothership. A moment later, the universe streaked past the window. A tunnel of stars and planets quickly turned into pure black, and then empty white nothingness, a place so far from the rest of the universe, nothing existed.

"What is this? Where have you sent us?" Kraven cried, abandoning the fight to stare out the window.

"It's right where you belong. The middle of nowhere," Finn said. He pulled the cables that connected the wormhole generator to the ship, then yanked it free. As Kraven stalked him, Finn punched in the coordinates to a small blue world with big green continents in a galaxy called the Milky Way, then pointed the machine toward a little town called Cold Spring, New York. He felt a rumble and a flush, and heard another tunnel open just as Kraven swatted him across the room.

"No!" Lincoln shouted.

Finn crashed against the wall, and everything got dark and wobbly. All he knew was Kraven was hovering over him, his mandibles snapping, his back legs cracking, and a thick string of saliva poured out of his mouth. His black eyes were no longer empty. They were full of rage.

And then everything melted around Finn.

28

He woke up in his bed. Everything was quiet and still. He wrestled himself from under a blanket and ran to the mirror on his bedroom wall. When he pulled off his shirt, he saw that the machine was gone. There was no scar, no burn marks, no evidence that it was ever there at all.

He padded to his bedroom window. Outside the sky was gray and cold. The mothership was gone, as was its feeding spike. He wondered if maybe he had dreamed it all—Kraven, Highbeam, the invasion, the unicorns. Pre'at—but then he spotted a couple of men in black suits poking around the neighborhood in dark sunglasses. The military tanks were still parked out front, along with Dax's spaceship. It wasn't a dream.

There was a light knock on his door, and then it opened. Mom wrapped him in the biggest hug of his life. Kate followed her and did the same.

"You've been asleep for two days," his sister said.

"Everyone has been worried sick," Mom explained.

"Really?" Finn cried. He sniffed his armpit. Yep, at least two days.

"C'mon! If you hurry, you can say goodbye," Kate said.

"Goodbye?"

He followed them outside and into the garage. A rousing cheer met him when he stepped through the door. Everyone was waiting. Several of the kid robots hoisted him on their shoulders and marched him around.

"All right, kids, set him down. Earth boys are fragile, and if you break him you have to buy him," Highbeam said.

When he was back on his feet, he hugged the robot.

"Glad to see you're alive and kicking," Highbeam said.

Pre'at approached and shook his hand. Hers was sweaty and kind of disgusting, but he suffered through it. She was so happy to see him. In fact, it was the first time he had ever seen her smile.

"Is it over?" he asked.

"I believe it is," she said. "The unicorns took care of the ground invasion, and from what I'm told you sent the ships packing."

"The last thing I remember was Kraven trying to kill me," Finn said.

Lugnut stepped forward. "Yeah, we took care of him," the kid robot cheered. "We demo-moded his butt all over that ship."

"And we used the wormhole generator to come home," Dax said.

"The new version is one hundred percent rift-free," Pre'at bragged.

"Kid, you saved the world," Highbeam said.

"You actually saved the universe," Dax said.

All the kid robots cheered.

Mr. Doogan stepped through the crowd. Finn hadn't noticed him at first, but there he was, smiling at him. He patted the boy on the back. "Well done, Mr. Foley," he said with a wink. "I suppose we can tear up those expulsion papers."

"I'll buy you a new mug," Finn promised.

Doogan smiled. "Deal."

The deputies gave him pats on the back, though Dortch promised to keep a careful eye on him. When Day scolded him, he laughed and promised it was a joke.

Highbeam placed the wormhole generator in Finn's

hands. "Kid, some folks are eager to get home," he said, gesturing out the window. Finn saw a herd of unicorns milling up and down the street. Kate was speaking to Blood Reaper.

Finn went out and joined them.

"You have brought a new passion to our hearts, Earth girl," the unicorn said to Kate. "I speak for all of my brothers and sisters when I say Kate Foley will forever be known as one of us, a sister of the Merciless Herd, stallion of the bloody hoof, clan member of the terrible horn. We will celebrate the savagery of this battle. Every year a bonfire will burn in your honor. The name Kate Foley will be heard in songs for all eternity. We will tell our colts and fillies of your bravery and how blood stained these streets. You must do the same."

"I definitely will," Kate said as she pulled part of a locust's wing out of Blood Reaper's mane. "I might leave out the parts about the blood, if that's okay."

All the unicorns bowed their heads and whinnied in unison.

Deathkick brushed up against Finn. "It was my honor," she said.

Finn thanked them and used the generator to open a tunnel to Haven. Moments later, thousands and thousands of unicorns raced into it and disappeared.

"I'm a sister of the Merciless Herd!" she said. "Lucia is going to be so jealous."

Pre'at said her goodbyes, along with the other aliens whose weapons had helped them win, then they all climbed aboard Dax's spaceship. Goldplate gave Finn a hug and did her best to herd her twenty-five kids in as well.

Dax gave Finn a wink. "Thanks for taking care of the big guy," she said, gesturing toward Highbeam. "Sometimes he gets himself into trouble he can't get out of. Usually I'm the one that has to save his butt."

Highbeam's digital face frowned, and Dax laughed. She waved goodbye and went inside her ship.

Mom and Kate said their goodbyes, as well as Mr. Doogan, leaving Highbeam and Finn a chance to talk alone. The robot bent down to one knee and put his hand on Finn's shoulder.

"I'm going to miss you," Finn said, fighting back tears. He tried to hide them with his shirtsleeve, but they came anyway and streaked down his face. He let it all out, every tear he had kept at bay, for his life, his dad, and now for a friend he would never see again. He cried until there were no more tears left.

"C'mon now, partner," Highbeam said. "My programming won't let me cry, but I feel an ache in my fluid pump. I'm gonna miss you, too."

"Everyone I love leaves," he said.

"Not everyone, kid. You know, it might seem like the world has dealt you a bad Pono hand—"

"What's Pono?"

"It's a card game, but with explosives and lots of running. It's complicated," he said. "But the point is that sometimes when you think you can't win, you look down at your cards and realize you've always been on top. Finn, you've got people who love you. You've got friends who really care. Don't push them away."

Highbeam stood to his full height and looked around at the neighborhood.

"You know, Earth isn't so bad. If I'm ever around these parts again, I promise to stop by for a visit."

"If I'm ever on the other side of the universe, I'll do the same," Finn said. He reached into his pocket and fished out the transmitter, then tried to hand it to the robot.

"No, you keep it. Could be useful."

Highbeam took the wormhole generator from Finn. His digital face formed a beating red heart, and then he turned and got on the ship with the others. The hatch door closed, and the ship's engines roared. A second later, it was hovering off the ground. A wormhole appeared in the sky and the ship zipped into it, and then they were gone.

"Did they just leave?" Julep said as she and Lincoln rode up on their bikes.

"Yeah," Finn said.

"It's cool. We already got to say goodbye to everybody," Lincoln said.

"Where's your dad?" Finn asked him.

"He's helping Nadia and Seth move out," he explained. There was a slight grin on his face. "So the world is safe again. What do you want to do?"

"Nothing," Finn said.

"I'm with him," Julep agreed.

29

Six months later

The days that followed were not easy. Finn, Julep, Lincoln, Mom, Kate, and all the others were questioned over and over, by the men in the black suits, the FBI, the police, and about a thousand other government officials who wanted to know everything they knew about aliens, giant talking bugs, weapons, and robots. Eventually, they all went away and left the family alone. One nice thing they did was to protect their identities so Finn and his friends and family were never on TV or the newspapers, but the neighbors knew. The kids at school stared at him in awe for months. Mr. Doogan went to work one day and found almost two hundred "World's Greatest Principal" mugs waiting for him, all gifts from his grateful students. But eventually things went back to normal.

Summer vacation came, with hot and sticky temperatures. Julep and Lincoln found Finn lying in his backyard on most days. The grass was cool on his skin.

"So, did you experience any paranormal activity last night?" Julep asked him. She lay down next to him and pushed her glasses up.

He tried not to look at her. She still made him feel happy and barfy at the same time.

"I told you it wasn't paranormal. It was just a creaky pipe," Finn said. A week earlier, Mom complained about hearing moaning coming from the toilet, but when Finn took it apart, he found it was just clogged.

Julep had a different theory.

"Finn! Cold Spring is one of the most haunted towns on the East Coast," she said. "I have like fifteen books on the subject."

Lincoln lay down next to them. He couldn't help but laugh.

"You are the weirdest people I have ever met," he said.

Kate came out, sporting her royal wave and wearing a tiara Mom bought for her at a dollar store.

"Still doing the unicorn princess thing?" Lincoln asked her.

"I am a sister of the merciless herd!" Kate stuck her

tongue out. "Are you guys going to spend the whole summer out here doing nothing?"

"Maybe," Finn said. "We're in Cold Spring. What else is there to do?"

"Tell Mom I went to Georgia's. The new episode of *Unicorn Magic* hits the internet in an hour."

A moment later, she was gone.

Finn looked to the sky, half expecting to see the Plague mothership hovering overhead. He felt a little ache for Highbeam.

"I wonder what he's doing right now," Julep said, seemingly reading his mind.

"Probably wondering why he had twenty-five kids," Lincoln said.

Suddenly, there was a flash of light in the corner of Finn's eye. He and the others sat up, straining against the energy that was burning in the middle of his lawn. It was shaped like a perfect circle and spinning so fast the edges were on fire. A figure stepped through it, and when Finn's eyes focused, he saw a tall being with orange skin and a metal ridge running down both sides of his head.

He didn't have a nose. He did have a long, busy mustache that hung down like handlebars on a bike. But the weirdest thing about him was his clothes. He was dressed like a cowboy: jeans, leather chaps, boots with spurs, a red handkerchief tied around his neck, and a tall cowboy hat. On his chest was a silver star engraved with the image of an hourglass, and he was spinning a lasso. Finn realized the lasso made the portal, though he wasn't sure how. The portal disappeared the second the stranger collected the rope and hung it from his belt.

"C'mon, kids. Time's a-wasting," the being said.

"Who are you?" Finn asked.

"My name is Zeke, and I am a Time Ranger."

"A what?" Lincoln asked.

"Are you from outer space?" Julep pressed.

"Yes. Well, no . . . kinda. It's hard to explain. I'll clear it all up later. Right now, we need to get moving. We don't want to make the others wait."

"We're not going anywhere with you," Lincoln said. "We don't even know you."

Zeke turned to Finn. "This is about your dad, Asher Foley. I have information about him for you, but to get it you have to come with me."

"My dad? You know my dad? How?" Finn said as he got to his feet.

"Uh-oh, you've got that smile on your face," Lincoln said to Finn.

"What smile?"

"The one where you do something dumb and get us into trouble," Lincoln said. "You're not really going with him, are you?"

"He knows something about my dad," Finn said. "You two stay here. I'll be back as soon as I can."

"You're a dope! This orange weirdo from a space rodeo just popped up in your backyard and you're going to run through his flaming portal, just like that?" Lincoln scowled. "I hope you don't think we're coming with you!"

"Everyone has to come," Zeke said. "You're all part of this."

"Part of what?" Lincoln demanded.

"Time is unraveling. The whole universe is in jeopardy, and you three might be the only ones who can fix it," Zeke said.

"I'm in!" Julep took Lincoln's hand and dragged him to his feet.

"Now you've both lost your minds!" Lincoln frowned and threw up his hands in surrender.

"I'm glad you're all in agreement," Zeke said. He spun his lasso in a circle. Finn watched it go faster and faster until the rope caught fire. A shimmering doorway appeared inside the ring.

"Get your cameras ready, boys," Julep said. "I think we're about to see something amazing."

She snatched Lincoln and Finn by the hands, and together they leaped into the mysterious portal.

Acknowledgments

Writing a book is not something you do all by yourself. There are hundreds of people through the course of a lifetime who inspire stories and characters. To them I say thank you. If you see yourself in these pages, I hope you feel I treated you with love. I would also like to express some special gratitude to my editor, Wendy Loggia at Delacorte, for her patience as I fell into this wormhole, over and over again. A big thanks to everyone at Delacorte. Your passion for my book is out of this world! (See what I did there?) Thank you to my agent, Alison Fargis, and her team at Stonesong, who have always believed in me, no matter what crazy ideas come out of my head. And to my son, the real Finn, who inspired every page.

About the Author

Michael Buckley lives in a part of New York known for evil robot attacks. Luckily, his son, Finn, and their magical wonder dog, Friday, are at his side. Together, they defend the peaceful and simple people of Brooklyn from the metallic, brain-eating horde. Somehow, during all the fires and chaos, Michael found time to write twenty books. They include the Sisters Grimm series and the NERDS series. You might like them. A lot of people suffered while he wrote them. It was time he should have dedicated to fighting the robots.

Do you have more questions? Do you have tips on fighting evil robots? Take a peek at michaelbuckley writes.com, his weird videos on YouTube, and his Instagram page at @buckleystopshere.